THE BIGGEST VICTORY

OTHER BOOKS BY ALFRED SLOTE

STRANGER ON THE BALL CLUB

JAKE

THE BIGGEST VICTORY

Alfred Slote

J. B. LIPPINCOTT COMPANY / PHILADELPHIA AND NEW YORK

U. S. Library of Congress Cataloging in Publication Data

Slote, Alfred.
  The biggest victory.

  SUMMARY: The only thing Randy enjoys about baseball is
having it over with so he can go fishing, but his father insists
that he participate on the school team.

  [1. Baseball—Stories] I. Title.
PZ7.S635Bi   [Fic]   76–37389
ISBN–0–397–31252–0   ISBN–0–397–31210–5 (Lib. bdg.)

FOR MARILYN E. MARLOW

CONTENTS

THE BIGGEST VICTORY

1 · MAYBE TOMORROW

DAD USED TO say that time was on my side. Maybe tomorrow I'd learn to hit a baseball. Maybe tomorrow I'd start catching a ball cleanly, start throwing on target. All I had to do was give myself time, be patient. After all, I was a McElroy and all McElroys are baseball players.

Dad used to say that and Dad used to believe it, but I always knew different. I knew I'd never be a good baseball player. I wasn't coordinated; I was stiff, muscle-bound, plus I never knew what was going on while I was playing. While I was watching a game, I could see it all, tell it all, but when I was in the game I never knew what to do. So naturally I hated playing.

11

The fact is I may have been the only player in the Arborville Baseball Leagues who *liked* sitting on the bench. I would have been happy to suit up for every game if only I didn't have to play, but in the Arborville Leagues—at least in the twelve-and-under leagues—everyone in uniform has to get in the game for at least one inning. So Mr. Stevens, our coach, always put me in right field with an inning left to play. Whether we were ahead, behind, or tied, in I went. My team—the Burton Bakers—dreaded my appearance. So did I.

One day at the beginning of my last season in organized baseball we were in a close one with the Baer Machine team. They had a great pitcher—Bob Skanecki—but he wasn't pitching now. I guess we were slumping or something because we can usually beat Baer Machine when Skanecki's not pitching. But this time we were a run behind as we came into the top of the sixth—which was the last inning of regulation play in our age group, the eleven-year-old league. The Baer Machine coach, walking by our bench to the third-base coaching box, spoke to Mr. Stevens.

"Hey, Don, you haven't played Randy McElroy yet."

Mr. Stevens, who was about to put me in, grinned and said: "I was hoping you hadn't noticed, Phil."

A groan went up from our bench. I felt like groaning too. I had been happy until then.

"OK, Randy," Mr. Stevens said, "get out in right field and try not to get hurt, huh?"

Everyone laughed. I turned red. I'm a great blusher. All the McElroys are, though I'm the only one who has to do it regularly. I got my glove and trotted out to right field. Ed Palwicz who had been playing there gave me a friendly thump on the rear.

"Protect yourself at all times, man."

"I know," I said.

Right field was a good place to play for me. Of course, it got dangerous when we had a fast pitcher going and they had a right-hand batter with slow reflexes up. Or if there was a lefty up who could pull the ball. . . . But most of the time right field gave you a nice sense of privacy.

In that inning, no one hit the ball out to me and I relaxed and thought about other things, which meant fishing. I was crazy about fishing then, and I still am now. I thought about the old bullhead who lived in the Huron River. He was about three feet long. Well, at least two. I'd seen him there for two summers now and he was King of the Bullheads. Wise, old, and big. I tried to catch him every time I fished the Huron, but he was as smart as a trout. He may have been part trout, but old Mrs. Gonder who fishes down there says fish don't get mixed up like dogs. Though I don't see why not.

Anyway, that old bullhead and I had a date and I thought about him almost all the time, especially in right field.

"Hey, Randy! That's three outs."

Laughter curled around the field and, red-faced again, I ran in as fast as I could. The Baer Machine team was on the field already.

"Dreaming again," Mr. Stevens said to me with a little smile. "What are we going to do about you?"

I didn't say anything because there was nothing to say,

and nothing he or I could do. My father insisted that I play Little League baseball. Baseball and McElroys went together. Dad had played high school and college baseball in Arborville. His older brother Ned who lived down the block from us had also played high school and college baseball in town. My cousin Teddy who is only two years older than me was one of the best young pitchers in Arborville, and then there was me. For eleven years old, I was big and I was strong, but I couldn't hit, I couldn't field, I couldn't throw. Even my two older sisters, Nan and Julie, were better coordinated than me, and my kid sister Mary could outhit me right now.

All of this drove my father crazy. Here I was, the only boy in his family, and I wasn't performing the way a McElroy boy was supposed to perform.

Dad wouldn't accept it. And so every spring, right as rain, he'd fetch out gloves and balls and we'd start warming up. He was thinking: maybe this would be the year. And if not this year, then the next. It was always . . . maybe tomorrow.

"Way to go, Jimmy."

I looked up. Even sitting on the bench, watching the game, I was out of it. Our lead-off man in this inning, Jim Felch, had just hit a hard single through the box. Everyone began to talk it up. Now maybe the roof would fall in on the little left-hander who was the number two pitcher for Baer Machine.

I didn't talk it up. For one thing, it was occurring to me that if the next batter—Otto Gehring—got on, there was a good chance I might have to bat. While I wanted us to catch up and beat Baer Machine, I didn't want to get up to the plate and make a fool of myself and my father too.

Otto Gehring stepped up to the plate. Otto was our first baseman and he had a funny batting style. He crouched so much he looked like a huge turtle. Somehow he managed to hit balls out of that crouch.

This time, though, he drew four straight balls. The pitcher was tiring. Our whole bench started yelling. Me too. I was rooting for our center fielder Ray Panello to get a big hit. A single would bring Jimmy home from second and tie the game up, but a double would bring Otto all the way around and win it. That would mean I wouldn't have to bat.

The Baer Machine coach was out at the mound talking to the left-hander. The little pitcher looked unhappy with himself for walking Otto. I've noticed that is the way with pitchers in our league. They will be breezing along with perfect control and then suddenly they can't find the strike zone, and it is hard to know why they have suddenly become awful. You can't see it coming.

The Baer Machine coach left his pitcher in there and we knew why. He was saving his ace Bob Skanecki for the Belden Hardware team. Baer Machine had a chance to beat us with that little left-hander, but no chance at all to beat the Hardwares without Skanecki. The Hardwares were the best ball club in our league.

The little pitcher was sweating now. Up till now he had pitched a good game, but now it looked bad for him. He was coming untied, like a ball of yarn.

His first pitch to Ray was low for a ball. Our bench was making a lot of noise. His second pitch was in the dirt, but their catcher Rob Franks blocked it out front and forced Jimmy Felch back to second.

Mr. Stevens gave Ray a "take" and Ray moved his bat back and forth, trying to make himself look small. It worked. The next pitch was over his head for ball four. Bases loaded. Nobody out. The noise reached to the sky. A fly ball ties it, a single wins it. Who's up?

Steve Turner, our number three pitcher, was up. Turner was only a fair hitter. After him, there was Mark Borker our catcher, and then . . . me.

"C'mon, Steve," I shouted, "we need a hit."

A single would win it for us. A single would get me off the hook.

"Give it a ride, Steve," I shouted.

"Way to talk it up, Randy," said Davey Lundgren, our second baseman and number two pitcher.

"Pitcher's going up, up, up," Ollie Stevens shouted.

"Nuts," Doodie Brown said glumly, "pitcher's going out. Look."

We stared, and slowly our voices died. The Baer Machine coach was yanking the little lefty and bringing in their number one pitcher, one of the best pitchers in the league—Bob Skanecki.

This meant Skanecki would only have five innings of eligibility in their next game against the Hardwares, but I guess their coach figured a bird in the hand was worth two in the bush.

We watched silently as Skanecki walked to the mound. He was big and he was strong and he threw with confidence. He grinned as he threw his warm-up pitches.

Here he was, bases loaded, nobody out, and enjoying himself. I envied him.

The ump allowed him ten warm-up pitches and then Skanecki was ready to face Steve Turner. Steve choked way up on the bat. Even so it would be hard to get around on Skanecki's fast balls.

"Be smart up there, Steve," our coach said, and I guessed he was telling Turner to take the first pitch. Skanecki might not be as cool as he pretended. He was a high fast-baller, but now with bases loaded and nobody out he might try to aim the ball. He might get too careful and walk someone. And a walk meant a tie game.

Skanecki, however, soon settled any doubts about how cautious he'd be. Pitching from a stretch position, he blistered a fast ball by Turner for a strike.

"Just meet it, Steve," Ollie called out.

"OK, Steve," our coach shouted down, "you know what to do with it."

Steve choked up even more on the bat. Skanecki waved his third baseman in and the first baseman too. They were looking for the squeeze, but I did not think Mr. Stevens had signaled for one. I wouldn't have, if I had been coaching. Not with no one out and Skanecki throwing high hard-to-bunt fast balls. A grounder had a better chance of bringing in a run, especially against a tightly drawn up infield.

Skanecki fired, high and fast. Steve swung and missed. Baer Machine shouted. They were confident; Skanecki was going to mow us down.

The big right arm flashed downward again and Steve,

swinging with two strikes on him, went after a very high pitch. He had no chance of hitting that ball, but with two strikes and that ball coming so fast, it was hard to know what else to do.

"That's all right, Steve," our coach called out, "we'll get him now. Mark, come here a second. . . ."

Mr. Stevens conferred with Mark Borker. Everyone was watching them, including Skanecki. After he was through talking with Borker, Mr. Stevens huddled with Jimmy Felch, our runner on third.

Everyone knew what was going on. In the eleven-year-old league, nobody fools anybody else. We all know about the same amount—very little. Anyway, it was the ideal situation for the suicide squeeze. Jimmy Felch, while not the fastest man on our team, was strong and a good slider. Mark Borker, while not our best hitter, had a good eye. He could bunt pretty well.

The only problem was Skanecki and those high fast balls. They're hard to bunt. You pop up a lot of those, and with Jimmy coming down the line, a pop-up could mean an easy double play and the end of the game.

Still, it was worth the risk.

Mark stepped in. The noise quieted down. You could sense the tension everywhere, on the field, on the benches, in the stands. I glanced up at the stands. Dad and Mary were sitting together. Dad looked grim. He was probably wishing he was eleven years old again and up at the plate. I wished he was, too.

"Be tough, Mark," Mr. Stevens called out, and clapped his hands.

Skanecki went to his stretch position. The third baseman and first baseman were way in close. Skanecki started to throw. Jimmy went down the line. Mark squared around and bunted, but the ball rolled foul, just missing Jimmy Felch, who hopped over it.

Close. Skanecki wiped his brow. Mr. Stevens clapped his hands. We sat back on the bench. My hands were sweating. I didn't like baseball when it got this way. I wished I was fishing.

The squeeze was still on. With the third baseman playing way in close, Jimmy Felch took a long lead. The shortstop bluffed a move to third, forcing Jimmy back a little. Skanecki fired. Jimmy didn't get as good a jump, but he was coming anyway. Mark squared around. He bunted and again it rolled foul.

I think we were lucky that time though. The third baseman was in on that ball and Jimmy would have been an easy out at the plate.

With two strikes on the batter, the Baer Machine infield moved back a little bit. The squeeze was off, but they still wanted to make the play at the plate.

Skanecki fired and Mark swung. A high infield pop-up. Nobody could come home on this one. Skanecki called for it himself and caught it halfway between the mound and first.

Two down. One out away from victory. The Baer Machine kids were talking it up.

"Who's up?" someone on our bench asked.

"Number nine man," Mr. Stevens called out.

"That's you, Palwicz."

"Nope," Ed said, "Randy's in for me."

"C'mon, McElroy, for cripe's sake, get up there."

19

"C'mon, Randy, a little bingle, baby."

"You can hit him, Randy."

"Wake up, Randy. Swing a bat, Randy. . . ."

I jumped off the bench and began swinging a bat. Mr. Stevens was annoyed. He thought I hadn't known when I batted, but I knew. I guess I was just sort of hoping to the very end I wouldn't have to bat and make the last out.

Ollie Stevens put his arm around me. Ollie's the coach's son, our number one pitcher, and our best all-around player. He hates losing.

"Randy, man, you can hit this guy. All you got to do is bring your bat around and let the ball hit it. It'll fly out of there. Be tough up there. . . ."

They were all talking it up for me, but their hearts weren't in it. Even Ollie's heart wasn't in it. Everyone knew the game was as good as over. Baer Machine knew it, Mr. Stevens knew it, I knew it too. I removed the doughnut from the end of the bat and walked up to the plate. I glanced at my father and Mary up in the stands. Mary looked bored; Dad was looking at me. There was no expression on his face, but I had a good idea how tense he was. Mom hated for him to go to games, but he loved baseball and now that he was too old to play, he wanted me to . . . .

"C'mon, Randy," the ump said, "let's get in there."

Rob Franks, the Baer Machine catcher, grinned up at me. "It looks like you don't want to bat, Randy."

"I don't," I said, and heard the ump laugh.

On the mound Skanecki grinned at me. I was his meat and we both knew it. All he had to do was get it over. If I was lucky I'd pop it up. Most of the time I just swung and

20

missed. . . . I knew what I should try to do. Don't swing hard. Just make contact with the ball.

Make contact with the ball? That was the answer. If *I* could get hit by the pitch. I wouldn't mind getting hit, even by Skanecki. I had a lot of meat on me; it would tie up the game. Still, you're not allowed to stick your hand over the plate. Skanecki would have to be a little wild.

I crouched at the plate.

"No stick, Bob," the catcher called out.

"Easy man, Bobby."

"No batter there."

Skanecki went to his stretch. Hit me easy, I prayed. But the pitch was a fast ball over the heart of the plate.

"Strike," the ump shouted.

"C'mon, Randy," Mr. Stevens called out, "that was right down the pipe."

"It only takes one to hit it, Randy," Ollie called out.

"Just a little bingle, Randy baby," Doodie begged.

"No stick, Bobby."

"He's waiting for a walk, Big Bob."

Skanecki went to a stretch, looked at third. They were keeping Jimmy close at third. The third baseman was practically on the bag with him. They didn't want Jimmy stealing home.

Skanecki threw to the plate. The ball was inside and not too fast. I nudged my elbow out over the plate, but it missed me. I couldn't even hit a baseball with my elbow!

"Strike two," the ump called.

The Baer Machine team was really yelling now. The game was in the bag. Our team was silent. Only Jim Felch on third shouted down, "C'mon, Randy, swing."

21

Swing? Swing and I'd strike out. I had to get hit by the pitch. This time I'd get my elbow into it. No, I'd get my whole body into it. I wouldn't care what happened, how much it hurt. I had to get hit.

The noise stopped. Skanecki went to the stretch, reared back, and fired. I stuck my left elbow way out across the plate. But the pitch was outside. I pulled my arm in.

"Strike three," the ump shouted. And he grinned at me. "It caught the corner, Randy. . . ." And then he added: "Do you want to wreck your arm in a Little League game? Don't ever do a thing like that again."

It would have been pointless to tell him it wasn't my fishing arm.

The game was over. Baer Machine was mobbing Ska-necki. On our side of the diamond, Ollie Stevens was kicking at the bats in frustration. Jimmy Felch, looking grim, walked by me without a word. No one looked at me. No one talked to me. In the stands, my father was still sitting, letting everyone else leave first. It would be a long ride home, I thought.

2 · A LONG RIDE HOME

It's only a ten-minute car ride from West Park to our house. You go up Huron to Forest, then along the university's women's athletic fields onto Washtenaw Avenue, and then up Washtenaw till you get to Ferdon and our house. There's an even shorter way to go, cutting through town, but my dad likes driving by athletic fields—even girls' fields. Once in a while we'll stop to watch a field hockey game. On Sundays the foreign students play cricket and rugby there, and Dad and Mary will go watch that.

This time, although there were lots of games going on at the women's athletic fields, Dad didn't even glance over. He looked straight ahead, grimly, and we drove in silence.

That's one way to tell the losers from the winners in kids' baseball. The winners' cars are full of noise and they're usually heading for Dairy Queens. Losers go straight home in silence.

When we got to Washtenaw, we were stopped by a red light. Mary, in the back seat, was humming.

"Could you be quiet?" Dad said.

Mary shut up. I looked out the window. I didn't mind her humming. Maybe I should have. It was crazy . . . as if Dad had lost, as if Dad had struck out, not me.

Dad tapped his fingers against the wheel.

I looked out the window. Here it comes, I thought.

"Randy, what happened to you at bat?"

"I . . . don't know."

"Why didn't you swing?"

"I don't know."

Mary piped up, helpful as usual. "Ollie said you were trying to get hit by the pitch and didn't have the nerve. He said it was too bad because if you'd gotten hit the Bakers would have tied the game and maybe you'd be out for the season with an injury too."

"That'll be enough out of you, Mary," Dad said.

"I was just saying what Ollie said."

"I'm not interested in Ollie. I'm interested in Randy, and why he won't swing a bat at the plate."

Thank God the light changed, and we moved forward with the traffic. Now if we could only not get hit by another stop light, we'd be OK. But sure enough, as we came up to Washtenaw and Hill, the light turned red. I winced.

Dad turned to me. "Why didn't you swing?"

"I guess because I didn't think I could hit the ball."

"How'll you know if you don't try?"

"Dad, I've tried a thousand times. I can't hit. My only chance to help the team is to get a walk or get hit."

Dad was silent. The light changed, we moved again and made the right turn at Ferdon. "That," he said softly, "is the saddest thing I've heard in all my life."

"Maybe. But it's true."

"It's not true, Randy. You're my son. I played baseball as a kid. My brother Ned played baseball. Your cousin Teddy is a fine ball player; there's absolutely no reason why you can't be a good baseball player."

"I'm not. That's the reason. I'm not."

"That's not a reason. But I can tell you why you're not good *yet* . . . and that's because you're developing more slowly. Kids don't grow at the same rate. That coordination will come to you. I can tell you one thing, it won't come to you without practice. You're not getting enough practice. Don Stevens throws you in the game for two minutes. How can you be expected to hit a ball?"

"Dad, he's a good coach."

"I'm not saying he's a bad coach. All I'm saying is you're not getting any hitting practice. What are you doing tomorrow morning?"

"I was going fishing."

"Forget it. You and I are going over to the park and have some intensive batting practice."

"Aren't you going to go to work?"

"I'll take the morning off."

"Dad, this is crazy. I want to go fishing."

"I know you do, Randy. And I know why you prefer fishing to baseball. It's a lot easier for you. No one's watching, no one's yelling at you, you don't really have to perform to have fun. I understand all that. But I also understand this. Fishing is just that, fun. Nothing more. Baseball is fun and a little bit more."

"A little bit more hell," I said.

"If you call training for life 'hell,' then that's what baseball is, Randy. But baseball is going to teach you something none of the bullheads in the world will teach you."

"What?"

"How to play with a team. How to cope with pressure. How to fight back when you're down. How to be a good sport when you win and when you lose. Baseball *is* life, Randy, and don't you forget it."

There didn't seem to be very much I could say to that. I wanted to ask why wasn't fishing life, too? Alone in the woods, by the river, no noise at all, just you and a fish, you and the unknown below the surface of the water. Why couldn't that be life, too?

But it was silly to argue with Dad when he got this way. So I didn't, and we drove the rest of the way in silence.

My cousin Teddy was in our driveway shooting baskets when we arrived, and that told me he'd won tonight. He's a snotty athlete type who thinks he's better at everything than everyone else. The only trouble is that he is. Whenever he does pretty good, he's always in our driveway, waiting to be asked what happened.

Despite all that, I liked Teddy. I liked to wrestle with him too. Although he was two years older than me, I was almost as strong as he was. Whenever our wrestling got a little rough, he'd always stop it and say: "Easy now, Randy. Got to watch out for my meat arm." Or something dumb like that.

Right now he was arcing one jump shot after another through the basket. When we pulled up, he stopped and came over to my side of the car. I shook my head, hoping he'd get the message not to ask. He got the message, of course, so he asked.

"How did your game go, Randy?"

I made a face at him. Teddy laughed. "What did you lose by?"

"Three–two."

"Tough. How did *you* do?"

I didn't think Dad could hear me, so I said quietly: "I hit two home runs and made an unassisted triple play."

Teddy laughed, whirled, and threw up a long hook shot. He almost made it. He followed it in, grabbed the ball, jumped, and it swished.

"Can I shoot, Teddy?" Mary asked.

He bounced the ball to her.

I carefully did not ask Teddy how he did, but he proceeded to tell me anyway, and this my dad did hear.

"I pitched a two-hitter, and one hit was an infield single."

"What was the other hit?" Dad asked.

"A fluke double over the left fielder's head," he said, grinning. "Want to go a little one-on-one, Uncle Jack?"

"No," Dad said. "What did you win by?"

"Four-zip. Have a shot anyway."

He bounced the ball to Dad who twirled it in his hands and put up a two-handed set shot. Old-fashioned but effective, it swished.

"You'd never get away with that in a game, Uncle Jack."

"Why not?"

"Too easy to block. Try it again."

Dad laughed. My dad was six foot one, Teddy was about five foot five, but he was always challenging Dad to basketball games. Uncle Ned was a salesman and not home very much, so Teddy was over at our house a lot. He liked playing ball with my father. They were both very competitive. My father was a younger brother, so was Teddy. Teddy's older brothers, Ralph and Howie, were both good ball players, too, but nothing like Teddy. It would have been all right if Teddy and I weren't so close in age, but as it was, my father was always drawing comparisons.

I left them in the driveway playing one-on-one, with Mary watching and muttering that she wanted to play too.

I went in the living room and sat down. Mom was out back. Nan and Julie were upstairs in their rooms. I could hear their radios going.

Mom called out: "Is that you, Jack?"

"No, it's me. Randy."

Mom came in. "How did it go?" She searched my face. "You lost, didn't you?"

I nodded.

"Did you play?"

"Aw, Ma, you know I have to play. Everyone has to play."

Mom sighed. She didn't come from a family of athletes. Athletics didn't mean a thing to her, and she didn't know why it meant so much to Dad, but because she loved him, she went along with it.

"I'm sorry. Did you not play well?"

"I never play well. What's for supper?"

"Was it really bad?"

I nodded. "How long before we eat?"

"About twenty minutes." She looked at me for a while and then shook her head. "You have time for a shower."

"I'm gonna practice with my fly rod."

"All right, Randy," she said. She came over and started to kiss me on the head.

"I'm OK, Ma," I said angrily, and twisted away. I ran upstairs and shut my door. Outside I could hear the thump-thump of the basketball against the backboard and Teddy shouting and Dad shouting.

I didn't take out the fly rod. I just lay down on the bed and listened to them playing together.

My sister Nan is a member of a synchronized swimming group at the Swim Club where we belong so that's what we talked about at the supper table. Afterward, I dumped the garbage which was my chore while the girls did the dishes. Mom and Dad sat out on the porch while Mary and Julie went down to the basement to watch TV. I went up in my room, turned on my radio, and looked over my trout flies. I had ten, six of which I'd tied myself. After the baseball season was over we were going up to Uncle Ned's cottage on Grand Traverse Bay. There were lots of good trout streams around there. Uncle Ned liked to fish and he and I went out together a lot. I thought trout fishing was the best thing in the world. Uncle Ned had taught me to fly fish, which is hard to do.

I liked to practice fly casting in our yard, but I didn't feel like it tonight. It would only get Dad mad anyway. To his way of thinking I should be swinging a bat, not practicing with a rod. Well, that was tomorrow morning in a nutshell. Swinging a bat and no fishing. It would be grim.

I turned off the radio. It was only eight thirty. I thought I'd go down and watch TV; then I thought no, Dad and Mom will be down there and the baseball game will get rehashed and nuts to that. Better stay in my room.

I picked a book off my shelf. It was one I'd read twice already but it was really a good story: about a bunch of French kids living in the country and there's a big old one-toed fox that lives there, too, and an old man who plays the violin. I really liked that story. I would have given anything to be a French kid living near a one-toed fox. French kids didn't have to play baseball. Well, maybe they had to play other things. I bet every kid in the world has to do something to please his father that he hates to do. That's what's wrong with being a kid. I hope when I'm a father I won't make my kid do something he hates. I know I won't make him play baseball.

I laughed. Maybe I'll make him fish.

I lay down on the bed and looked at the printed words, and then something came between me and the book. It was my mom and my dad, I could hear them talking on the porch below my window. At first I couldn't hear their words separate from each other, but then by concentrating I could.

They were talking about me. They were talking about Little League baseball. And Mom was doing most of the talking.

"I don't want him coming home like that again, Jack. It's not that important. It can't be that important."

"You're making it important, Ellen," my dad said. "With Randy, it's not important. It's a matter of practice and timing. Tomorrow morning I'm going to work out with him—"

"Do you have to?"

"Yes. I'm tired of his looking like a damn fool at the plate."

"Does it bother Randy as much as it bothers you?"

"Of course it does. It has to."

"Then why don't you let him drop out of baseball? Is it really so important that he be a good baseball player?"

"But he can be one, Ellen. It's a matter of practice. . . . Why do you think Teddy is so very good? He's playing every day."

"He's playing every day because he likes it. Randy doesn't like it. Why should he play it at all? I'll tell you, Jack, I think the idea of your brother having boys who are

31

good ball players is killing you. You're trying to make Randy be like them. He's not. He's got other talents, other skills."

"Name one."

"Fishing. Reading. He likes to read. And reading's a much more important skill than hitting a baseball. You're really pushing him too hard and I don't like it. As a father you're being a younger brother, you're competing with Ned and his sons and I don't like it. And furthermore, I won't have it."

Dad was silent. "Ellen, you're entitled to your views. I think you're making a big thing out of this. I don't want Randy to be a major leaguer—"

"That's very nice of you."

"I've had enough," Dad said, and a second later I heard the inside door slam, and then silence.

I put the book down. I couldn't see the words anyway. They were blurry.

There was a knock on my door. It was Nan. She stuck her head in.

"Randy, what's the matter?"

"Nothing," I said.

"You're crying."

"No, I'm not."

"Of course you are. I'm not blind or deaf. What book are you reading? It must be a very sad story."

"It is," I said.

3 · A GRIM PRACTICE

AT FIRST I thought my private special batting practice wouldn't be so bad. Except for a man way out in deep center field training his Irish setter, or shouting at it anyway, Sampson Park was empty. It didn't really start filling up till eleven, and by eleven I hoped Dad would be sick of me and would let me go down to the river.

"C'mon, Randy," he said, "wake up."

"Sorry. I didn't know you were ready."

"I've been ready for five minutes." Dad was dressed in a sweat suit and wore an old Michigan varsity cap. He looked like a ball player. I was really proud every time I saw him throw or catch. He had an ease about him.

He turned around and looked at Mary who was supposed to be fielding for us. Mary was lying down at shortstop chewing on a blade of grass.

"What do you think you're doing?"

"Waiting for Randy to hit one."

"Get up and look like a ball player."

"When do I get a chance to bat?"

"Later. This practice is for Randy."

"Everything's always for Randy."

"The back of my hand will be for you unless you get up."

Mary got up slowly. I guess it was pretty boring for her. I know that if it was me out at shortstop, I'd be chewing grass, too.

Dad looked at me. "Bend your knees a little more, Randy. Straighten out your back a little. Good. How's that feel?"

"Fine."

"Now a level swing. Nope . . . you're swinging up. A level swing. That's better. Now that's all you have to do. And watch the ball. When it arrives, hit it. It's the simplest thing in the world."

Simple if you can do it, I thought, impossible if you can't.

"Don't try to guess where I'm going to put the ball. Just hit it where it is. OK, eye on ball, bat back, elbow up, relax. You're tense. Relax up there."

Relax, I ordered myself. Relax.

Dad studied me for a moment more and then he pitched. He threw all kinds of pitches. Fast ones, slow ones, half-speed pitches. He threw them low, high, inside, outside, over the heart of the plate. He could put a ball anywhere he wanted to.

And I swung. I was under orders to swing at every pitch, no matter where it was. I swung at the high ones, I swung at the low ones, I swung at the right-across-the-heart-of-the-plate ones. And nothing happened. Oh, some I popped up. Some I fouled off. Some I missed completely. In a few seconds, we had a collection of eight balls lying within fifteen feet of me. A shambles of hitting.

"OK," Dad said, never discouraged, "gather them up."

I threw the balls back at him. He tossed one at Mary to make her happy and kept three in his glove, one in his hand, and the others around the mound.

I took off my batting helmet and wiped my face. Out in center field the Irish setter was running in happy circles around his master. A flock of birds soared overhead, and at the swings little kids were going up in the air with shrieks of laughter.

"OK, Randy," Dad said, "let's go at it again."

I put the batting helmet on. It clamped down heavy and hot. Dad looked down at me. "Set?"

"Yes."

As he was about to pitch, I heard a shout. "Hey, Mr. McElroy, you need any fielders?"

We both looked around. It was Ollie Stevens and Doodie Brown bicycling across the field. They had gloves and a bat with them.

"Sure," Dad said, and waved them to the field, "we need all the help we can get."

35

He turned to me. "OK, Randy, let's show your team-mates you can hit."

Dad thought it would help me that Ollie and Doodie were here. He thought I'd rise to the occasion. I'd be a competitor the way he was, the way Teddy was. I felt a little sick.

"Bang 'em out, Randy," Ollie said.

"OK, here we go, Randy," Dad said. He threw the fattest pitch ever thrown in the history of baseball. I knew he wanted me to look good. So I tried to knock the stuffings out of it. I popped it up.

"Wait for it to get there, Randy. You're lunging. Just wait. That ball will get to you soon enough, and when it does, then you whip that bat around. Then you'll smack it for a home run."

The next pitch he threw me was not so fat and I missed it.

"You're swinging stiff."

The third pitch was a half-speed over the heart of the plate. I topped it into the ground. The next pitch was high and inside. To my "power," or where my "power" should normally be. I pulled it foul into the trees near the tennis court.

"Wait on it, Randy. Wait on it."

Then he threw me another great fat pitch. It floated up like a basketball. Wait on it. Wait on it. Wait on it.

For once I did wait on it. And I brought my bat around and there was the ringing smack of wood on a ball. The ball took off for deep center and landed there and kept rolling. . . . Doodie was chasing it, but so was someone else. "Red," the man shouted, "leave that ball alone. Red!"

But the Irish setter had scooped up our ball, shook his big head around playfully while he got a better grip on it, and then took off with his master in pursuit.

"Red," the man shouted, "Red, bring that ball back. Red."

The last we saw of Red was his big red tail disappearing behind the hill, and a moment later his master disappeared, too.

Dad laughed. "Well, maybe you hit that one too far, Randy."

"They throw them harder than that in a ball game, Mr. McElroy," Ollie said. "If you want to give Randy practice, you better throw them hard."

Dad was irritated. I could see it, the way his mouth tightened. "I'm working on Randy's timing, Ollie. The hard pitches will come later."

"Yeah, but he won't see fat pitches like that. He'll get the wrong timing."

I privately agreed with Ollie, and I knew Dad did too. The only reason he was throwing fat pitches to me was that he wanted me to look good in front of my teammates.

"Would you like me to pitch some?" Ollie offered.

"Maybe later. OK, Randy, step in. Now that dog is gone, you can hit some more out there."

He threw and there were fat pitches among them, but I didn't hit another good one like that. In fact, I didn't hit one good at all. Mary lay down at shortstop, and Doodie sat down in left field. Only Ollie didn't give up on me.

"C'mon, Randy, hit it."

So I tried a little harder. Swung a little harder, but I never really got a good piece of the ball again. Dad was getting mad at me. He knew I was trying. I was trying to do everything he told me, but I wasn't hitting the ball.

Finally he gave up. "Ollie," he said, "get up there and show Randy how to hit."

I gave Ollie the bat and went out in left field with Doodie. Mary stood up at shortstop.

"How do you like them, Ollie?" Dad asked.

Ollie blew a bubble-gum bubble. "Any way you can throw them," he said.

Dad laughed. He threw Ollie a curve that Ollie just blinked at. Doodie laughed. "What's the matter, Ollie?" he shouted. "That looked pretty good."

"Throw another one like that, Mr. McElroy," Ollie said.

Dad threw another curve and Ollie missed it by a mile. "One more," he said.

Dad obliged and threw another one. Ollie struck out. Then Dad served up a mixture of pitches. Some fast, some slow, some curves, and he even threw a knuckler at Ollie. And Ollie fanned on almost all of them. The balls hit against the wire mesh backstop and lay there. At first it was funny, and I think Ollie liked it, but then I realized, and I guess Doodie did, too, that Dad wanted him to look bad. He wanted to make Ollie look as bad as I had looked.

It wasn't pleasant. After a few more minutes I couldn't

take it anymore and I asked Dad if practice could be over. I wanted to go fishing.

"What about me?" Mary asked. "When do I bat?"

Dad looked at his watch. "It's late. I've got to shower and get to the office. I'll pitch some to you another time, Mary."

"But you said I could bat, Daddy."

"We'll do it tomorrow."

"I want to do it now."

"All right. Randy, pitch some to her."

"I'm going fishing," I said. "I've had enough baseball."

Ollie, who had been very quiet up to now, said to me: "You're scared your sister can hit better than you."

I saw Dad watch me, watch for my reaction. I laughed and said: "I think she can."

I knew Ollie wasn't mad at me in particular. He was upset about looking so bad at the plate, and he wasn't going to take it out on my father who made him look bad, but on the rest of us who'd been witnesses to it.

"Let's see," Ollie said. "Let's see if Mary can hit better than you. I'll pitch to you, Mary," he said.

"You can pitch all you want," I said. "I'm going home."

I started to leave.

"We're all going," Dad said quickly. "Mary, you'll bat another time."

"I've got nothing to do today," she whined. "Can I go fishing with Randy?"

"That's up to Randy."

"No. She doesn't like to fish."

"Yes, I do."

"You don't. But I'm not going to argue with you. You can come with me."

"Get the balls together then," Dad said.

"What about the ball the dog got?"

"That dog was a pretty good fielder," Ollie said.

"If he could only bat," Dad said.

"I bet he can bat better than Randy," Ollie said.

Ollie was trying again. It hadn't worked with Mary, now he was comparing me to a dog. How silly could he get? Dad was silent; he looked at me. I knew he wanted me to do something. Get sore . . . or something, but it was just plain silly and Ollie was my friend. I'm not a fighter, I'm big enough and strong enough, but Ollie's my friend and just because he was sore at my dad and the rest of us, was no reason to fight him.

"Well," I said, "there's only one way to prove something like that. Stick a bat in his paw."

Even Ollie had to smile and Doodie laughed. Dad shrugged. "Let's go home," he said.

4 · SKIPPING STONES ISN'T FISHING

THE HURON RIVER isn't a good fishing river. It isn't even much of a river to look at. It's not wide, it's not deep, it's not pretty. The only thing the Huron's got going for it is that it's here. And it's our only river.

Part of the reason the river's a mess around Arborville is that they lowered the water level to build the bridge for the new parkway connecting the northeast and southeast parts of the city. Then they couldn't get the water level back up without spending a lot more money. So where it used to be all water, there's a lot of islands, bushes, trees, and snags. Any fish that can get where he's going has got to be plenty smart.

Which is what my old bullhead is. Smart and tough because he has survived the lowering of the water level, plus a lot of steel hooks, and lots of other things fish have to avoid in order to survive.

My old bullhead lives downstream of Dixboro Dam, which is a smart place to live because the banks are steep there and not many people are willing to climb down the banks to fish.

Most everybody parks their cars along the shoulder of the road upstream of the dam, or alongside the railroad siding near the dam. What I do is lock my bike up on the dam bridge and climb down the steep banks.

Mary and I were coasting down Geddes Hill together toward the tracks that separated the town from the river. A small dirt road ran along the river on the other side of the tracks. That's where cars were parked and where people fished.

"Hit your brakes," I shouted back to Mary. "It'll be bumpy going over the tracks."

She couldn't do anything more than nod, she was going too fast. Her right hand held her rod. I had told her to keep it in her left so she could apply all the force of her right hand to the brakes, but you can't get a little kid to understand a detail like that.

We both hit the tracks going too fast, but Mary held on, and she was actually grinning as she bounced up and down on her seat. A tomboy type. Maybe she'd be all right fishing. We braked into the dirt road and turned right and then it was easy pedaling till we reached Dixboro Dam. There were about a dozen people fishing off the dam and among them was my friend Mrs. Gonder. She had her grandson Sam with her. Mrs. Gonder was about eighty years old, I think, and a great fisherman. Sam was nine years old and a pain in the neck. Right now Sam was skipping stones and Mrs. Gonder was sitting in her folding chair reading the paper while she fished. Her red and white bobber was about fifteen feet out in the water, and Sam's stones were skipping near the bobber.

I biked up to where she was sitting. She looked up and smiled. "Well, I was wondering when you'd show up today."

"I had to play baseball. This is my sister Mary, Mrs. Gonder."

"Hello, child. You a fisherman too?"

"Fisher*woman*," Sam said, and threw another stone. Mary watched him out of the corner of her eye.

"Getting anything?"

"Lots of bites but no fish. Not with Sam here."

"How come you're not fishing, Sam?"

"I got no rod, that's why," Sam said disgustedly.

"Ha. He means he left it home."

"Aw, Gramma."

"Maybe Mary would share her rod with you, Sam," I said.

Mary gave me a dirty look.

I grinned. "She likes to share."

"No, I don't," Mary whispered furiously.

Sam was interested though. He dropped his stones and came over and examined Mary's rod. "What kind of rod is that?"

43

Mary looked at me with that pained "Do I really have to talk with him?" look.

"Has anyone been catching anything, Mrs. Gonder?"

The old lady pointed across the river. "They been catching some carp over there. I think they been catching them with their hands the way they're hanging down over the water. You goin' after your catfish again?"

"I guess so. You want to come?"

"Lord, no. Those banks are too steep for me. I got trouble enough trying to fish here with Sam throwing them stones."

"Aw, Gramma, stones don't hurt fish."

"A' course they don't hurt 'em, child. They save their lives. Ever'time your gramma is about to catch a fish you throw a stone and scare that fish away to freedom. Stones hurt a fish? Stones is a fish's best friend."

I laughed. The best thing I could do for Mrs. Gonder would be to get Sam off her back. I could put up with him better than she could. After all, I was fishing for fun, she was fishing for food.

"Sam, you want to come fish with us?"

"You gonna let me fish, Randy?"

"Sure."

"Can I, Gramma?"

"Don't you bother Randy none."

"I won't bother him."

"Don't throw no stones either."

"Nah, I won't throw stones."

"You help Randy catch that old catfish. They make good eatin'."

44

"We'll see you later, Mrs. Gonder."

"If he bothers you now. . . ."

"I'll send him back."

"No stones, Sam."

"Aw, Gramma. . . ."

We climbed over the side of the dam bridge and started down the downstream bank.

"How come you call it a bullhead and Gramma calls it a catfish?" Sam asked.

"I don't know. It's the same fish."

"It don't look like a bull, do it?"

"No, I guess it looks more like a cat."

"So why don't you call it a catfish?"

"I don't know. Careful here, both of you."

Mary fell first and started tumbling down. Sam, who had great balance and didn't have to fall, decided it looked like fun and he came rolling down behind her.

"What's the matter with you guys? Do you want to get hurt?"

"This is fun," Mary said, pretending she'd fallen on purpose.

"Yeah," Sam said, and rolled up to a tree at the edge of the water. "Come on, Randy, you roll too."

A great start, I thought. Although I didn't know it, worse was yet to come. Sam was absolutely fearless. He'd be a gymnast or a sprinter. Mrs. Gonder said he was all the time getting into trouble at school and watching him now I could believe it.

The two of them were staring into the water when I finally got down there.

"What do you see?"

"A dead fish," Sam said. "This river is polluted. Look at him."

It was a dead bluegill.

"C'mon," I said, "let's get going."

They followed me along the trail that wound between bushes. The ground was soft and soggy. We stepped over roots and vines and chunks of old bark. It smelled good here. Damp and fresh, like woods and berries. There were little red berries halfway up the embankment. They were tart-tasting but when you were hungry they tasted good.

Behind me, I could hear Sam whispering. "Hey, are you really Randy's sister? You don't look like him."

I glanced backward. Mary's lips were pressed shut. She was determined to ignore him. I laughed.

Sam saw me. "Hey, Randy, how far we going?"

"Just a little further."

"What's wrong with it here?"

"The old bullhead don't live here."

"How do you know where he lives?"

"I've seen him where he lives."

"How do you know he wasn't just visiting?"

Mary giggled.

"What's so funny?" Sam asked her.

"Bullheads aren't people. They don't visit," she said.

"How do you know?"

"Everybody knows that."

"I don't know that. And neither does Randy. Do you, Randy?"

"Shsh. . . ." I said. "We're here. That's where the old

bullhead lives. Right by that old tree lying in the water."

We stood there and listened to the water lap up against the uprooted tree. An old plank had drifted up against the tree and nudged it with each lap of the water. It was quiet here, sheltered. Twenty feet out, the river ran swiftly, making white water where it hit snags. It flowed fast from where it came down from the dam, but this was a little backwater.

"Lemme use your rod," Sam said to Mary.

"I'm gonna use it first," Mary said. She was as tough as he was, if not a little tougher. She was a McElroy all right. Sam would just have to get used to it.

"What kind of bait you got?"

"Worms."

"There ain't no worms around here."

"We brought them from our house."

"Lemme see your worms."

While the two of them examined the worms I'd dug out of the compost heap in our yard, I walked out onto the fallen tree and examined the spot where the old bullhead lived. I couldn't see him now, but I'd seen him just about every other time I'd been here. The old plank bothered me, but I don't suppose it bothered the bullhead. By now he'd be used to a river filling up with junk. It would be just another thing he could hide under.

"Randy, would you put the worm on my hook for me?" Mary asked.

"Ha! You scared of worms, ain't you?" Sam asked, grinning.

"I'm not scared," Mary said. "I just don't like to touch them."

"You scared all right," Sam said.

"Both of you be quiet. I'll bait your hook but then I want you both to be quiet."

"What for?" Sam said. "Fish can't hear."

"They can hear better than you."

"How do you know?"

"I *know*."

"How?"

"Scientists have made tests on fishes' hearing."

"Yeah. Well, suppose the fish flunked the test."

I ignored him and gave Mary back a baited hook. "Fish over there."

"Why can't I fish here?"

"Because I'm fishing here. There's no room for two people."

"Are there any fish over there?"

Sam giggled. "She sure don't know anything, does she, Randy?"

"Not much. Go and take turns with the rod. Go. Move."

Mary didn't look happy but she went and Sam went with her. Sam watched her closely and critically as she cast out. I prayed her line wouldn't snag on a tree or I'd be a half hour getting it unsnagged. It didn't. It floated onto the water and her sinker took the hook down and left her white bobber on the surface. Mary looked very pleased with herself.

"I can do that," Sam said. "Gimme the rod."

"Not yet," Mary said.

I left them to bicker while I got my own rod working. I cast out from shore about ten feet which let my hook go down right over the bullhead's nest, not far from the old plank. The worm went down slowly, gently, moving just enough to draw the old guy's attention. You never want to surprise a fish; you want to get him curious. Not scared, just interested. Everything's got to be slow and quiet. And it was. The only noise was an occasional car on the road, an airplane high in the sky. The river ran fast in the middle and the shadows of the tall trees rippled black and gold on the water.

I held my breath. A black shadow glided across the spot where my worm dangled. It could have been him. He'd seen the worm, and now he'd swum off to think about it. This was his spot, his home, he lived here. He was no visitor. Someone else was the visitor—me. I was poking into his house. He'd think about it, try to remember what it meant because a big old bullhead like him hadn't lived that long without knowing what that dangling thing meant. He knew it wasn't good. Out of his fish past he'd have a fish memory. Memory of pain, of being frantic, of twisting and turning while the edge of iron bit into his mouth, twisting and turning till somehow the iron came loose and he was free—bleeding, hurt, but free and swimming as hard as he could for clear water.

Maybe fish don't think. Maybe it's only people who do. But, as Sam says, you never know.

I waited. Somewhere down there the bullhead was also waiting. It was like a dance between two people who couldn't see each other, who heard different music but who knew they were going to dance together.

The water moved. I saw him then—big and black and full of whiskers, showing himself to me, letting me know he knew I was there. But that was silly. He was looking at the worm. He glided right up to the worm and looked at it, thinking it over, trying to remember something about it, something he knew about it. He wasn't curious anymore; he was recalling the past. Don't let him remember, I thought. Get him curious again, irritated. I wiggled my rod ever so slightly and pulled it toward me. After a moment's hesitation, he came with it, drawn by a magnet he knew nothing about. Then, all of a sudden, he looked up. I swear to God that old fish looked up right through the surface of the water at me. He looked me right in the eye. I froze. I didn't move a muscle. I held my breath. This was it. He was going to take that worm right now. After defying me. Defying all humans. He would dart at it, seize it in his powerful jaws and I'd—

"Seven!" Mary shouted.

"Six!" Sam yelled.

The bullhead vanished.

"You kids," I shouted. "What's the matter with you?"

They were skipping stones on the water. Neither of them was fishing.

"If you don't want to fish, go back up to the dam and throw your stones up there." I was so mad I'd forgotten it was my idea to get Sam off his granma's back.

"There's no good stones up there, Randy. Hey, Randy, you watch this time and you see who skips the most."

Before I could tell him to go jump in the river, Sam sidearmed a stone across the water. And I found myself counting the stupid jumps: one, two, three, four . . . and it sank.

"That was a *bad* stone," Sam said.

"Watch mine, Randy," Mary said.

I felt sick at losing the bullhead and now here I was watching these kids skip stones. The only time I'd ever enjoyed skipping stones was up at L'Anse at the bottom of the Keewenaw peninsula, where the stones seemed to have a lot of iron in them . . . all those stones skipped ten, twelve times. But we weren't fishing then. We were just walking along the shore.

Mary threw. Her stone sank without skipping at all.

Sam started laughing.

Mary turned red. "That doesn't count," she announced.

"Why don't it count?"

"OK," I said, "that's enough. Both of you kids get out of here right now. I want you to go back up to the dam and stay there. You just chased away my bullhead with your darn stones."

"Where's your bullhead? Let's see your bullhead," Sam said, and he came running over the shore, jumping over a vine, with Mary a half-step behind.

"He's not here now, stupid. You scared him away."

"Maybe he'll come back."

"Not if he has any sense."

"There he is," Mary said. "I see him."

She was lying, of course, trying to get back at Sam for beating her in stone-skipping.

"Where?" Sam asked.

"Oh, he's gone now. But I just saw him."

"You didn't see him."

"Yes, I did. He was big and black and had big old hairy whiskers on him."

"You making that up. You didn't see him. She didn't see him, did she, Randy?"

"Get out of here, both of you."

"She's lying."

"I am not lying. I saw him right by that old tree. Right there."

"Right here?"

"Sam, where're you going?"

"I'm gonna see if she's lying or not."

Sam jumped out onto the fallen tree and scampered along it like a cat.

"Where'd you say you saw him?"

"Right there," Mary said, pointing toward the old wooden plank.

"I bet," Sam said. And then before I could warn him, he stepped onto the old plank. The plank went down, and so did Sam.

5 · I LAND A BIG ONE

I REMEMBER ONCE reading a story by Jack London. In this story people were sitting around in a log cabin up in Alaska arguing about how you would react if something really unexpected happened.

Well, sure enough, something unexpected happened. A crazy man came into the cabin with a rifle in his hand and wanted to shoot them. All the men in the cabin, including the guy telling the story, froze. They were paralyzed. The only one who reacted fast was a woman. The only woman in the cabin. I don't remember what she did, but she reacted fast and saved them all.

I guess the point of it was, you never know how you'll

react to the unexpected until the unexpected happens to you, and then you either react fast or don't.

That story by Jack London flashed in my mind the instant Sam fell in the river. I did *not* react. I just stood there paralyzed while Sam yelled that he couldn't swim.

"Just stand up," I said. "It's shallow."

But even as I said that, Sam went under.

It was a scream from Mary that got me moving. Sam was underwater. I jumped into the river and waded out to where he had gone down. The next thing I knew, I went down too. It was like stepping off a curb. I came up for air and then went down again to look for Sam. He was coming up in a chairlike position, staring at me, moving his hands in circles, like he was describing something to me. There were bubbles coming out of his mouth. I grabbed him around the waist and we both broke to the surface together. He started yelling, spitting, and flailing about with his arms. An elbow caught me on the jaw.

"Cut it out," I shouted. "I've got you. You're OK."

I had him, but he also had me and neither of us was OK. The bullhead's nest, I now realized, was nothing but a deep hole in the riverbed made when the tree was uprooted. There was nothing to grab onto. I couldn't swim with him hitting me in the face and screaming. And he was getting heavier every second.

Mary was standing on the shore, watching us as though she'd never seen two people drown before.

"Get something I can grab onto," I called to her. "Get a stick. . . ."

Just getting those words out took all the air out of me and down Sam and I went. We came up right away. Sam screamed and hit out. He was really panicked. I tried changing my grip on him, to get an arm across his chest and then sidestroke us both over to the tree. But every time I moved my arm, he grabbed it tighter and held on. We were both stuck. The tree was only a few feet away, but it might as well have been a hundred yards. I was treading water with legs that were getting tired fast.

"Here," Mary said.

She had miraculously found a long board. Where she found it, I don't know. But it was just the thing.

"Hurry," I gasped.

And then she did an incredible thing. I guess it was a scream from Sam who'd gotten some more water up his nose that did it. Instead of holding the plank of wood out to me to grab onto, Mary panicked and threw it at me. Well, she's a McElroy and has got the McElroy arm. The edge of the wood hit me in the forehead. I was knocked backward and that was all I saw or felt. Vaguely I heard Mary screaming and Sam screaming, but I couldn't see a thing. Everything went black. My head was swimming far away down river, away from my body. And I was certain Sam, too, was floating off somewhere.

The next few moments were a confusion of screams and voices and water hitting my face and the salty taste of what I knew was blood flowing down from my forehead. I was afraid to feel for it. I didn't even know where my hands were anyway.

Then I heard a man's voice close to my ear.

"Just let go of him, son. I've got him. He's all right. You'll both be all right."

It was the first I realized I was still holding onto Sam.

55

I let go, and sank downward immediately. The water cleared things up for me though. I opened my eyes. It was dark, but water-dark. Not crazy-in-the-head dark.

When I came up again, I saw a man I'd never seen before lying stomach down on the fallen tree, holding a hand out to me.

"C'mon now, you've had enough swimming for one day." He was actually grinning. So things had to be all right.

"Give me your hand and I'll pull you in."

I gave him my hand and he pulled me to the tree. In a second I felt the solid rough comforting feel of the bark.

"Just hold on till you get your wind back, then I'll give you a hand up."

"I'm OK."

"Sure you are. You got a nasty cut on your forehead, but you're OK. How'd you get cut?"

I looked over to shore. Mrs. Gonder was there and Sam was in her arms, crying, wet, but OK. Mary was standing there sobbing.

"I got it jumping in. I must have hit something."

"That means you dived in. You never want to dive in a shallow river, son. You're lucky you didn't break your neck. Got your strength back yet?"

"Yeah."

"OK. Now you give a little jump up when I count three. You're a big kid." I felt his hands under my arms. Big strong fisherman's hands. "One, two, three. . . ." I jumped and he lifted and a second later I was lying limp as a fish across the tree.

"Let's see that cut now."

I turned my face up to him. He took out a handkerchief, dipped it in the river and began wiping my forehead.

"Hmmm. . . . Better get you to a doctor. You may need some stitches there. Here, you hold the handkerchief tight against your forehead. Can you walk off?"

"Sure," I said, and stood up, almost falling right back in the river. He grabbed me and we both laughed. But my head hurt. Oh, how my head hurt.

"Just hold onto my hand, we'll move off slowly. You set?"

I nodded.

When we got onto the shore Mrs. Gonder threw her arms around me, and to my amazement she was crying too.

"Randy, are you OK?"

"Sure, I'm fine."

"You saved that good-for-nothing child's life. . . . And you got a cut."

"I'm OK. I really am. Thanks a lot, mister."

"Better thank the little girl, too. If she hadn't screamed, we'd never have heard and made it down here."

"Oh, that cut is awful. Sam, see what you did to Randy."

"I didn't do that to him," Sam said. "She did." He pointed at Mary. "She tried to hit us with a stick while we was drowning."

Despite everything I started to laugh. Sam, panicking, drowning, wild and wet, hadn't missed a thing. And now he'd tell the story to his friends the way he wanted to.

Mary burst into great sobs.

"C'mon, folks," the fisherman said, not knowing what to make of it, but sure we should not be standing around wet and bleeding. "Let's get Randy to a doctor. You got a family doctor, son?"

"No. We go to the University Hospital Emergency, most of the time."

"Well, let's go there then," the fisherman said.

I remember little of the climb back up the embankment, only that old Mrs. Gonder was hauling Sam along and scolding him, and I had to use one hand to fend off the bushes and trees because the other was holding the fisherman's handkerchief to my forehead. Mary was using one hand too because she had our rods in her other hand.

When we got to the top, a whole collection of people was waiting for us. A police car with a flashing blue light pulled up, and pretty soon Mary and I were inside it. I kept telling the policeman about our bikes and that we could bike over to the Hospital Emergency, but he told us not to worry about them.

I felt embarrassed to be driving to the Emergency in a police car with a flashing blue light. Mary sat next to me, small and scared, still clutching the fishing rods.

She only said two things to me that whole ride to the hospital: "Randy," she said, "I didn't mean it."

"I know that," I said.

And then a couple of minutes later, she said: "Randy, we left the worms there."

I said: "We still got the whole afternoon to fish in."

But we didn't. I didn't fish again for a whole week. That was pretty bad. But what made up for it was that I didn't have to play baseball for almost the whole summer.

All that came later. When we arrived at the hospital, I was certain we'd be let out in an hour or so. My clothes would be dry by then, I figured. An hour or so is what it usually took us in Emergency. A lot of my memories have to do with sudden trips to Emergency at the University Hospital: Mary swallowing a button, Nan falling off her bike, me falling out of a tree. Years ago doctors used to come to your house, but now almost everyone in Arborville runs to the hospital. And sometimes when you get there you think everyone in Arborville is there.

You sit and wait for them to call you and it's not as bad as you think, because when you see them bringing in people who are really hurt you think you're lucky.

But I'll say this for the emergency service at the University Hospital. They don't like the sight of blood. And if you come in bleeding, you really get the attention. Sometimes it's really wild. A bunch of young doctors practicing medicine for the first time, I guess, alongside a bunch of old nurses who don't think much of the young doctors, and there are the attendants who seem to be the only ones who care about you. They wink at you and tell you you're going to be OK and want to know how big the fish was.

I got examined right away.

"It looks worse than it is," I heard one young doctor say. "A butterfly bandage ought to do it."

"I'm for stitches," another young doctor said. "You'll end up stitching him anyway."

59

"Who's his mother?"

"She's not here."

"How'd you get here, son?"

"A police car brought him."

"Hit by a car? How'd you get all wet?"

"He fell in the river and then the police car hit him."

"Cops drive in funny places. That hurt?"

"No."

"What were you going after? Swordfish?"

"I think we ought to X-ray his head."

"What did you hit?"

"A piece of wood."

"Nice bump he'll have. We're going to give you a few stitches, son."

"You got to get permission, Dick."

A door opened. A nurse said: "We've got his mother on the phone."

"Go talk to her, Dick. Tell her we want to put in stitches."

One young doctor left; one old nurse came in. "Do you have a Blue Cross card, Randy?"

"Oh, come on, Nurse. This kid was out fishing."

"He's a hero. He saved a kid from drowning. You'll probably get your name in the papers. That ice still feel cold?"

"Yes."

"As soon as your mom says OK, we'll fix you up and you'll be on your way home."

The doctor who'd talked to Mom came back in. "She says OK. She's coming right over. There's nothing to worry about."

"He's not worried, are you, Randy?"

"No."

"Good. After this little prick, you won't feel a thing. Give me the ice. Here we go . . . there."

I didn't feel a thing. The doctor sewed me up, and I really felt OK. They gave me a room to sit in and Mary sat with me. She kept saying she was sorry and I kept telling her to forget it. Then the door opened and there was Mom, looking as though she expected me to be dying.

Mary went "Baw . . ." and ran to her.

"Now, now," Mom said.

I stood up.

"Randy," Mom said. She couldn't move to me because Mary was holding onto her, weeping. "Are you all right, darling?"

"He's fine," the young doctor behind her said. "Your son is a hero. He—"

That's all I heard. I guess standing up suddenly was a mistake. Or maybe it was seeing my mom, or maybe just the whole thing finally being over. Because all of a sudden everything started going round and round, and I felt myself falling, a long, long way down. . . .

I felt something cool and nice come up to meet me. It was the tile floor. And a long way off I heard the young doctor say:

"Now I guess we *will* X-ray his head."

And I remember thinking, just before I drifted off to sleep: This will get me out of baseball.

6 · REPRIEVE FROM BASEBALL

"I DON'T WANT to play baseball. Please, Dad, don't make me play. Please, please, please. . . ."

The words were somewhere else, outside of me, and there was another voice talking, and then my cheek stung, and the words died away, and the stranger who had slapped my face spoke:

"Focus on me, Randy. Focus on me."

I looked at him. A white moustache, blue eyes, shaggy eyebrows. An older man, his face was only inches away from mine. He was peering at me. How long had he been there?

The face moved away. The man stood up. "He's out of

it now, Mr. McElroy. A case of shock, a little delayed."

He was a doctor. And he was talking to my father who was standing in the middle of the room, looking enormous and worried. When Dad saw me look at him, he forced a smile onto his face, and came and sat down on the edge of my bed.

"How are you, Randy?"

"Fine."

The doctor harrumphed. "He's not fine at all. Jumping into rivers, diving into hospital floors. The child should have his head examined. Well, fortunately, we did just that, and you're all right, son."

"Can I go back fishing?"

"No, you cannot," the doctor said grumpily. "You're going to stay here overnight so we can double-check you. Then if you haven't scared all the fish in that poor polluted river, you can go back tomorrow and catch some."

"What about his stitches?" Dad asked.

"You'll bring him back in ten days and we'll take them out. But don't ever let me catch you diving into rivers again, young man. Not while I'm running this emergency service. . . ."

And with a few more harrumphs and pretend-grumpy remarks, the doctor walked out and left Dad and me alone. Really alone, because neither of us knew what to say to each other. Dad felt queer, I could tell, and embarrassed. And because he felt embarrassed, I did too. In another room a radio played music, and you could hear the usual hospital sounds: carts being wheeled, a distant voice, an elevator stopping, a loudspeaker page for a doctor. . . .

Finally, I asked where Mom was.

"She took Mary home. She'll be right back."

"How's Mary?"

"She's finally stopped crying."

"Good."

Dad smiled, reached out to rub my head and then pulled his hand back as if he'd been burned. "Does that hurt, Randy?"

"No. It feels numb, that's all."

"You've got quite a bump."

"I guess. Do you know what happened to our rods?"

"Mother took them home."

"We left our bikes on the bridge."

"The police brought them home already. There's nothing to worry about, Randy."

With that the conversation died, like a quick breeze on a hot August afternoon.

A train whistled down the track by the river. The hospital was near the river. I wondered if the old bullhead was still there or had taken off, trying to put a few hundred miles between him and the two lunatics who had jumped into his nest.

Dad got up and walked around the room and ended up at the window. He stared out, and when he spoke, his back was to me.

"When you were coming to, a little while ago, Randy, you were saying things. Do you remember?"

"Something about baseball, but I wasn't sure I was the one saying it."

"You were." He paused. "Randy, I didn't mean to force you to play baseball."

When I didn't answer, he said: "I thought you'd like it after a while."

"I do like it, Dad. I just don't like playing it. I'm no good at it. I will never be any good at it."

I waited for his line: "Maybe tomorrow. . . ."

"Maybe . . . you won't ever be," he said.

I was stunned. I'd never seen my father give up on anything before. And while I wanted more than anything else in the world to have him give up on me as a baseball player, I was scared now to see him quitting. Quitting and my father didn't go together.

"Dad, it wasn't as bad as that."

"No, let's not either of us stall. Would you like to get out of baseball, Randy?"

There it was, finally. A fat pitch that I could hit, that would end the ball game once and for all. And I was suddenly scared to come flat out and say yes.

"Randy, be honest."

He said that, and I could hear echoes of every third base coach I'd ever had saying: "Be tough in there, Randy. Hang in there, Randy."

"Yes," I said.

"All right, it's settled. I'll call Mr. Stevens tonight." And then he quickly changed the subject. He talked about going up north in August, and how I'd have to teach him fly fishing because he was going to catch as many trout as Uncle Ned or die trying. He talked and talked and I listened.

Later, Mom came back to the hospital and Dad told her in a soft but unembarrassed voice how I was going to teach him fly fishing and how we were going to let baseball go.

Mom listened. She didn't rub it in. She just sat there and listened, and when he was done, she said: "Randy, people have been calling our house all afternoon. I think everyone in town knows about it. The newspaper called too."

"How did they find out about it?"

"From the police. And Mr. Simpson called to ask how you were doing."

"Who's he?"

"Why, he's the fisherman who saw it all happen."

"He didn't see a thing, Ma. He just saved us both."

"Did he? Well, that was nice of him." Dad and I laughed. Mom told me that Mrs. Gonder called, too, and was baking a pie and the newspaper wanted a picture of me and she'd given them one Dad took of me last summer holding three trout. The picture was taken up north.

"Oh, Ma, you shouldn't have given them that one. They'll think I caught those trout in the Huron River."

Mom and Dad thought that was funny, but I didn't. No fisherman would.

The next morning I was an official hero. Made official by the *Arborville News*. My picture was there, holding the three trout, and below it a headline said: LOCAL YOUTH SAVED FROM DROWNING. It was a really great story. They put two d's in Sam's last name, made him ten instead of nine, had us on the wrong side of the dam, had me fishing from a boat when I dived into the river and pulled him all the way to shore. They got Mr. Simpson's name in it, only they called him an eyewitness. If anyone was a hero, that man was.

When Mom came at noon to take me home, she told me the phone had been ringing steadily all morning. Neighbors, kids, Mr. Stevens had called; Mrs. Gonder had called three times. My cousin Teddy was waiting for me. He was going to blow his cornet when I got home. Everyone, she said, was very proud of me.

"But I think the one who is proudest is your father," Mom said, with a little smile.

"Did he tell Mr. Stevens . . . about baseball?"

"Yes, he did. He told him you were going to drop out."

"What did Mr. Stevens say?"

"He said they'd miss you."

I smiled.

"But that you were welcome to sit on the bench anytime. And he wanted to know if you'd be interested in scorekeeping for the team, and maybe even coaching at third."

I looked away. It was my turn to feel blurry around the eyes.

"Ollie called, and Jim Felch and Otto and Davey Lundgren. I think they all must have called."

"They're all crazy."

"I'm proud of you too, Randy. I bought fifty copies of the newspaper."

"What did you do that for?"

"I'm going to send a copy of that article to all our relatives."

67

"Aw, Mom."

"Just how often does a son of mine jump in a river to save someone from drowning?"

"It wasn't all that much. You're making it sound more than it was."

"I know what it was, Randy. Mary told us what happened. She told us exactly what happened, including what she did, and how you told everyone you struck a board by yourself. Please be nice to her, Randy. She's still upset and blames herself for everything. Don't tease her."

"Tease her? Mom, I owe her a Dairy Queen for getting me out of baseball. She should have knocked me on the head years ago."

Mom laughed. "Be kind just the same," she warned.

The whole family, except for Dad who had to go to work, was waiting for me at the house. And the first thing I saw and heard was my smart-aleck cousin Teddy blowing his cornet for what he announced was a "hero's welcome."

Nan kissed me and Julie kissed me and they made a big fuss, and neighbors came out of their houses and shook my hand and made oohs and ahs about my stitches and the bump on my forehead.

Teddy said I was going to be hard to live with from now on. I didn't deserve all that ink in the newspaper. Anyone would have done what I did. I told him to shut up. He wanted to know if I'd like to play one-on-one with him in the driveway.

"No one-on-one," Mom announced. "Randy's going to take it very easy until those stitches come out."

"Gee, Aunt Ellen, his stitches are in his forehead. They'll never get hit."

"You wriggle your forehead a lot when you're excited," Mom said. "I'm not taking him back to Emergency."

"Let's see you wriggle your forehead, Randy."

"Go jump in the river."

"No, that's your bit," Teddy said. He took out his cornet and blew some more noise and then Nan and Julie chased him home. Mom went inside to make lunch, giving me one more "don't tease Mary" look.

All this time my nine-year-old sister had been riding her bike in circles, embarrassed, wanting to say something but not knowing what or how. She reminded me of Dad.

Finally she hopped off her bike. "Do those stitches hurt?" she asked.

"Yes," I said.

She bit her lip. "No, they don't," I said quickly. "Where did you put the fishing rods?"

"In your room. I forgot to bring the worms back."

"That's OK. They'll start a colony there."

"Are you still mad at me?"

"No. And I wasn't mad at you then either."

"Randy, I don't know why I threw that stick. I guess I was scared."

"Forget about it."

"It was really that awful little Sam's fault. If he hadn't come along, everything would have been fine."

"That's right. It's all Sam's fault."

Mary looked at me and then burst into tears. As luck would have it, Mom stuck her head out the window at that moment and began to call us in for lunch. She took one look at Mary crying and began scolding me.

"Didn't I tell you not to tease her?"

"I wasn't."

"Then why is she crying?"

"I don't know why she's crying."

"Come in, both of you. Right now."

I rubbed my hand over the bump on the forehead, over the stitches. The truth was, I should have been grateful to Mary, but how could I explain that to her, and how would she ever understand it?

I decided I would buy her a Dairy Queen later in the day.

"Come on, dopey," I said to her, "let's go in."

Still crying, she went in with me.

7 · A HAPPY SUMMER

THE DAY I came home from the hospital marked the beginning of a happy summer for me and for everyone else
too.

The pressure was off me, and when it was lifted off me,
it went off everyone else, too. Dad no longer had to wince
when I took a called third strike, Mr. Stevens no longer
had to wince when he put me in the lineup, and Ollie,
Doodie, and the others no longer had to wince when I
trotted out to right field or lugged my bat to the plate.

At first the guys on the team pretended they were sorry
I'd quit. I liked them for pretending that, but after a
while they admitted it wouldn't be too hard to carry on

without me. They wanted to know how I'd saved the kid from drowning and I told them the newspaper story was full of mistakes and that a fisherman had pulled us both in. Doodie said I'd probably get a medal anyway.

"From who?"

"My dad says there's an organization that gives people medals who save people from drowning and things like that."

"Well, I didn't really save Sam, and what am I going to do with a medal anyway?"

"Hang it on the wall," Jim Felch said.

"I'd rather hang a big trout on the wall."

"Is that fly casting hard to do?" Ollie asked me.

We were all standing in my back yard where I'd been sending my line, without a fly and hook, out to different parts of the yard. I cast to the trunk of the apple tree, to our birdbath that squirrels were always knocking over. I shot a line to the top of the compost heap and dropped it between my mom's two forsythia bushes. I had gotten pretty good at fly casting—it's a lot like pitching to cor-ners, which, of course, I can't come near doing.

"You wanna try it?" I asked Ollie.

"Can I?"

"Sure."

"What's a rod like that cost, Randy?"

"About seventy-five dollars."

"Wow. Did you buy it?"

"Part of it. My dad chipped in some. You ever fly cast before?"

"No."

"Everyone look out then," Otto said.

"There's no hook on it."

"You could hit us with the stick."

"Listen to him. He calls it a stick."

"What do you call it?"

"A rod, dummy. A fishing rod."

"It's a stick just the same."

"Don't let him use it, Randy. Now what do I do?"

I showed Ollie how to cast, how to use your forearm and wrist, whipping the line back and forth while you got your aim so you could shoot your fly out and your line would fall straight and tight on top of the water.

"It's kind of cool, how you do it. Let me try."

"Look out below."

Ollie whipped the line back and forth and cast out. The line landed up in our apple tree.

"That's great for a flying fish," Jim Felch said.

"You think it's so easy."

"I wouldn't cast it into an oak tree."

"It's not an oak, Jim. It's an apple tree."

"Thanks, Randy," Ollie said. "Anyone who can't tell the difference between an oak tree and an apple tree oughtn't to be allowed to fish."

"You didn't know either."

"Sure I did. An apple tree's got apples and an oak's got acorns."

"Fun-ny."

"What did I do wrong, Randy?"

I got the line down and explained to Ollie that he was breaking his wrist too soon. He tried again. Missed the tree this time, but the line curled in a series of S's.

"Hey, this is hard."

"Let me have a try," Doodie said.

"Hold on. I wanna try it again."

This time the line got tangled up in the rod. "There's a rhythm to it," I said. "Just whip it back and forth a few times and you'll get the feel of it."

But Ollie didn't get the feel of it. Neither did Doodie, Jim, or Otto. So I took the rod back and showed them again. I had them pick spots around the yard and I laid the end of the line right on those spots.

"Trout hang out in small places, between rocks, by tree snags, so you got to be able to lay your fly right where you want or else you'll lose it."

"Is that what you fish for at the river?"

"No. There aren't any trout in the Huron."

"It's polluted," Doodie said.

"The fish don't know it's polluted," Jim Felch said.

"Ha," said Otto. "You think fish don't feel pollution."

"I don't know what a fish feels. But he doesn't call it anything like pollution."

"Fish don't have to call things anything, they just got to have the sense to stay away from it."

"How come there are so many people fishing down at the river then? What's Randy fishing for?"

"Bluegills, carp, pickerel," I said, "but I'm mostly after a bullhead who's about two feet long and giving me as hard a time as I'll ever get from a trout."

I told them about my old friend and enemy and how long I'd been after him and how he'd looked right at me —like he knew me—the day Sam fell in.

"When are you going after him next?"

"Tomorrow, I guess."

"Can we come?"

"We got a game tomorrow."

"Are you gonna come to our games, Randy?"

"I don't know."

"We won't mind," Doodie said. "We'd only mind if you played."

"Doodie," Otto said, "that's a rotten thing to say."

Doodie blushed. Ollie asked me if my stitches hurt.

"No," I said.

"Is that why you quit the team?" he asked, pointing to my stitches.

I shook my head.

"Why did you, Randy?" Jim Felch asked.

" 'Cause I'm terrible and I don't like playing."

Hearing Doodie say that was one thing, hearing me say it was embarrassing. A guy shouldn't be able to admit a thing like that in public.

Embarrassed, Ollie said: "You sure can wield a fishing rod, man. You mind if we come down and watch you fish sometime?"

"Heck, no." I hesitated, grinned. "You guys mind if I come down and watch you play?"

"Heck, no," Ollie said, imitating me, and we all laughed. "Fact is," Ollie said, "you're still on our team roster, Randy. My dad said there's no way we can drop you since you paid your buck to the Recreation Department."

"Now hold on," I said, "you won't put me in the game if I show up . . . 'cause if you do—"

They all laughed. I did too.

Everything was easy. The pressure was off.

There were two things I wanted to happen that summer. I wanted to catch the old bullhead (though I knew I'd be a little sorry when I did), and I wanted the Burton Bakers to win our league championship.

Now that I wasn't playing, we had a chance. The team was down to nine guys now. The other substitutes had gone on vacation, and what was left were nine regulars who wouldn't let their folks take a vacation until the baseball season ended in the middle of August. The team was playing heads-up, hustling, and steady baseball. They were now a well-knit team.

The eleven-year-old league had ten teams in it that summer. The best team in the league was the Belden Hardwares, from the central part of town, a poor neighborhood, and they were poor kids, but how they could play baseball! They were loose, undisciplined, talented, and large. The only thing that would prevent the Belden Hardwares from winning the championship was their pickup truck. The team was coached by a man who did maintenance work for the university and he drove an old Dodge pickup truck. Their guys rode to the games on the truck. The problem was that the truck broke down a lot. The only game the Hardwares lost that season was when their truck broke down and they got to Vets Park a half hour late and forfeited. Boy, were they mad. They won their next games by lopsided scores and walked to and from the games. They didn't trust their coach's truck anymore. But we'd heard they were back riding in it again. So we, along with other teams, prayed for spark plugs to come loose, for the radiator to spring a leak, for a flat tire. But when we played them, that truck rolled over to

Sampson Park in grand style and there they were: twelve or thirteen guys, banging bats against the sides of the truck as they drove into the parking lot, announcing to the world that the hottest team in Arborville was arriving. We were beaten before the first pitch was thrown.

The game against Belden Hardware was the first game I went to as a spectator. They won 6-2. Ollie pitched all the way and deserved better than he received. They only got six hits off him, but once they got on base you couldn't keep them there. They were fast. All of them. A guy would be on first. You'd turn around and he'd be on second.

I sat on the bench and kept score. I told everyone who was up next, and I tried to keep the Bakers on their toes.

The Hardwares had a big pitcher named Lonnie Malkus. I don't think he was as big as Bob Skanecki of Baer Machine, but when he stood out on that mound he looked like a skyscraper. And he liked talking to our batters.

"Hey, Ollie," he'd say, "I'm gonna throw some smoke at you. I'm a little wild with it, so look out, 'cause you're my pal."

And he'd pour his fast ball in there and there wasn't much anyone, even Ollie, could do. Mr. Stevens complained to the ump about Malkus talking to the batters but the ump said there was no rule against that. Then I remembered a rule because Dad and Uncle Ned had talked about it, that in the kids' leagues you couldn't bench-jockey the other team by name. I mean, you could say: "Hey, pitcher, your socks smell." But you couldn't say: "Hey, Ollie, your socks smell."

So we pointed this out to the ump and the ump shrugged and told Malkus not to call us by our names and Malkus grinned and said: "OK."

When Doodie got up there he said: "OK, little man, I'm gonna bend a curve for you. Don't you get cross-eyed watching it."

There wasn't anything we could do about his talking, and there wasn't anything we could do about his curve either. You just don't see many curve-ball pitchers in the eleven-year-old league, but Malkus threw curves that came toward you and curves that went away from you.

"Choke up, Doodie," I heard myself yelling, "follow that curve in. It'll break and you pound it."

Everyone on the bench turned to stare at me in amazement. In three years of Little League baseball I'd done everything wrong. Now I was telling everyone what to do. I blushed.

"Hey, that's all right, Randy," Davey Lundgren said. "Keep that chatter up."

We lost to Belden Hardware, but except for that one forfeit everyone else lost to them too that summer. We were winning more than we lost from other teams though. We beat Cornish Wire and we beat Marsh's Dairy. We beat the Exchange Club and Shumway's Cleaners. We walloped Mal's Standard Service who almost beat Belden and finished second last year. As July ended, and we went into the home stretch of August, Belden was in first place, Baer Machine (thanks to Skanecki's right arm) was in second place, and we were in third, only a game behind—and next week we were to play

Baer Machine for the second-place spot and a better perch in the playoffs.

Everyone felt good at the A&W Root Beer Stand where Mr. Stevens was treating us after a victory over Moore's Auto Supply. Mr. Stevens was feeling pretty proud of himself since he'd taken a chance and waved home the winning run from second on a single by Davey Lundgren.

"Very bold coaching, if I do say so myself," he kept saying. And then he winked at me and raised his glass and said: "Here's to our good-luck scorekeeper, Randy McElroy."

"You bet," Doodie said.

Ray Panello clapped me on the back.

Everyone solemnly agreed that you could date our winning ways from the time I dropped out of baseball. I agreed.

"I should have jumped in that river two years ago," I told them.

But that was only one part of why the summer was good. The other part was the fishing. I not only fished the Huron, but I biked out old Whitmore Lake Road and fished Whitmore Lake. And I biked out the Arborville-Saline road and fished Pleasant Lake. These were lakes I'd never had time to bike to before because we were always having practices or a game.

I fished with Mrs. Gonder a few times, but never again that summer with Sam. Mrs. Gonder told me Sam didn't like fishing anymore.

"He says you get too wet fishing," she added, with a chuckle.

The old bullhead was still there. I tried everything on him: worms, cheese, bacon, orange rind, grasshoppers, flies, artificial flies—but I couldn't get him curious and he certainly wasn't hungry. Either that or he had figured out in his fish mind what two-legged people with long poles meant. I had just a few more lures to try, and one of them was a little green frog that I had high hopes for. An old fisherman who said he used to catch bullheads in Ohio gave it to me.

I was going to try it the next time I fished the Huron, but then one day something happened and it looked like I wouldn't get a chance to fish again that summer.

There were only two games left before the playoffs. We had our second game against Belden Hardware, which we were sure to lose. And then we had our final game against Baer Machine. It was a four-team playoff and the team that finished in the second spot wouldn't have to play the Hardwares right off. It meant the team that finished in the second spot would have a good path to the finals. It would be either us or Baer Machine.

If we lost to the Hardwares but beat Baer Machine, we'd have second place sewed up. If we lost to them both, we'd be in third place and would have to play the Hardwares right away.

Mr. Stevens wisely decided to save our best pitcher—Ollie—for Baer Machine, and to pitch Turner for three innings and Davey Lundgren for three innings against the Hardwares.

"I want everyone to concentrate," he said at the team

meeting before the game. "If we hit Malkus and win—good. But our big game is Baer Machine. So don't do anything stupid out there like get hit on the head by a fly ball."

He was trying to remind us that we only had nine guys, and nobody had better get hurt in a game we probably couldn't win.

As I look back on it now, it was the wrong thing to have said. You never get hurt as long as you don't think about getting hurt. But think about it, and whammo! someone gets hurt.

Someone did.

8 · NEW COACH AT THIRD

THERE WERE THREE reasons we couldn't beat the Hardwares. One, they were a better team than us. Two, they had Lonnie Malkus pitching that day. And three, we were playing at the Buhr Park diamond where we'd never had any luck.

There are some diamonds that are like that. At Buhr, it always felt like we were batting uphill, running uphill, that the sun was always shining in our eyes. It was a hard luck diamond—the same hard Michigan clay as all the other fields, but its geography was all wrong for our club. Three out of the four games we lost that summer were at Buhr.

Our one hope of beating the Hardwares lay in a break-down of their pickup truck. Sampson Park, where we live, isn't so far from Buhr. We rode our bikes to Buhr and got there at 5:15. Mr. Stevens arrived shortly afterward with the equipment bag and we had infield and outfield practice. For the first time Mr. Stevens asked me to hit balls to the outfielders. I'd never done this before a game, but hitting fungoes was a lot easier than hitting pitched balls. So while he hit grounders to the infield, I hit fly balls to Ed, Ray, and Jim. And it got closer and closer to game time without any sign of the Hardwares. Our parents had arrived and were gossiping in the bleachers. The umps arrived and began staking the bases. Everyone was there except the Hardwares and our hopes kept rising. Without anybody actually saying it, we were all aware we would win this game very soon on a forfeit. Finally, with only five minutes left to go till game time, Jim Felch, grinning, said:

"Panello, you did a great job."

"What did I do?" Ray asked.

"Weren't you supposed to pull the spark plugs in their truck?"

"Hold on," Ed Palwicz said, "if they forfeit I get the credit."

"What did you do?"

"I put sugar in the gas tank."

"Well, you didn't put enough in," Davey Lundgren said, "here they come."

Our hearts sank. You could hear the Hardwares before you saw them. A wheezy coughing backfiring old truck, and their team banging bats against the sides, yelling it up. It was like the arrival of a traveling team of professionals.

"They do that to scare you," someone said.

"Well, they scare me," Doodie said.

"Heck, they're not that good. We can beat 'em," I said.

"Sure we can, Randy."

"Listen to Randy, he doesn't have to bat against Malkus. . . ."

"Randy's right," Mr. Stevens's sharp voice cut through our mournful chatter, "we can beat the Hardwares. Mark, warm up Steve. We're home team. We've never been home team on this diamond before. Maybe our luck will change. Randy, how would you like to coach at third base?"

Everyone was astonished. Mr. Stevens usually coached at third and the guy who'd made the last out in the inning before coached at first. The rule was you had to have at least one coach in uniform. If I coached third, it meant kids would be coaching both third and first. Almost every team had an adult at third.

"I think you can do it, Randy; you can pep these guys up. Let's go over signals. We'll make a take hands on hips. And we're all taking on 3 and 0 counts."

"How about 2 and 0 and we can't see Lonnie's fast ball?" Jim Felch wanted to know.

A sickly laugh went up. Alongside first base, Lonnie Malkus was kicking his leg high and punishing his catcher Joe Bibbs with fast balls. Mark Borker, our catcher, winced every time the ball smacked in Bibbs's glove.

"I bet he's got two sponges in there," someone said.

"The only thing worse than hitting against that guy is catching him."

"Borker would call for lots of slow balls, wouldn't you, Mark?"

"He's faster than Skanecki."

"No, he's not. He just looks faster."

"Fun-ny."

"He ain't even warmed up yet," a voice from third base said. Their third baseman, a husky kid named Junior Russell, had been listening to us. He was grinning.

This was a team, I thought, that liked to beat you before the game started. They couldn't be all that good.

"Listen, Junior," Ollie snapped, "wait till Turner pops a fast one in your belly button."

Junior laughed. "Turner couldn't break a pane of glass."

"How's your hospital coverage, Junior?"

"I don't use that stuff, man."

"What's your batting average, Russell?"

"A thousand, man, a thousand."

That broke us up, and even Mr. Stevens had to laugh. Then we huddled and went over our signals—making sure Junior couldn't see or hear us.

"Hands on hips is a take, bunt is when Randy takes off his cap."

"What cap?"

"He doesn't even have a cap."

"He'll wear my cap."

"Put it on, Randy. Let's see if it fits."

"It does fit. What've you got such a big head about, McElroy?"

"Quiet!" Mr. Stevens ordered. "Steal signal . . . Randy touches a foot. Either foot. Elbows and we hit away. Wipe everything out and hit away . . . Randy will put his hands on his knees."

Ollie looked at me, a smile in his eyes. "Randy, what's hands on hips?"

"Hit away."

"Touch toe?"

"Take."

"Cap off?"

"Only if it's not raining."

And that broke us up again. Well, between Junior's gags at third and my gags about signals, we were loose again, and looking back on it, I think that may have been Mr. Stevens's intention in having me coach third. We surely didn't have much of a chance of beating the Hardwares and no chance at all if we were tight. Our only hope (after their truck made it to the ball game) was to stay loose and hope for breaks. We had to figure our big game was the one against Baer Machine. But it would solve a lot of problems if we beat the Hardwares today. So I was coaching because the only chance we had to win was if we stayed loose.

The ump finished brushing off the plate. "Let's play ball," he called out.

"OK, guys," Mr. Stevens said, "no mistakes, no errors, everyone pays attention. Steve, just pitch your game. The guys will field for you."

"Let's get'm," Ollie said, and he lead the team off the bench.

Steve took his final warm-up tosses from the mound.

86

"These guys are *no* good," I shouted. Doodie took up the cry, so did Otto and Davey.

Mr. Stevens smiled down at me. We were the only two people left on the bench. "You know something, Randy. I have a feeling we may just beat the champs today."

"So do I, Coach."

Steve Turner is never overpowering. He doesn't throw as hard as Ollie who doesn't throw as hard as Lonnie Malkus who doesn't throw as hard as Bob Skanecki, but Steve is smart and he battles. He's also a good fielding pitcher. Because he doesn't throw too hard, he's never off balance on his follow-through. A good fielding pitcher is a must against a team like the Hardwares who are fast and can get lots of leg hits in the infield. They're also a big bunting team. They like to run and they're all fast.

No sooner did I think that than their first man up, Tommy Flagg, their shortstop, laid down a bunt on Steve's first pitch. We should have seen it coming, but we didn't. Doodie came in fast and gave it a good bare-handed try, but only a great snap throw would have beat Tommy, who sped across the bag at first long before the ball got to Otto. One pitch, one man on. The Hardwares were razzing us. It didn't look good.

"Keep him close, Steve," Mr. Stevens shouted.

Steve had a fair move to first. Otto was playing on the bag but Tommy Flagg moved off contemptuously, daring Steve to throw. Steve threw. Tommy dove back headfirst. His team razzed him. They were really a loose outfit.

Again Flagg took the long leadoff. Steve didn't know what to do. He stepped off the rubber to think about it.

He looked at Mr. Stevens who again called out to keep the runner close.

To me, Mr. Stevens muttered: "We can't let them terrorize us right off. That's their style."

Steve went to his stretch position again, glanced at first. Tommy was way off the bag, swaying back and forth, chanting: "C'mon, Pitch, get me out. C'mon, Pitch, throw it."

Steve whirled and threw. Otto jumped high in the air and made a great catch.

"Pitcher's going up, up, up, up. . . ." their bench chanted.

Steve wiped his forehead. Just the first inning. He'd only thrown one pitch. The sun beat down. The wind blew. It was such a bad luck diamond for us.

Finally Steve ignored Flagg and threw to the plate. Flagg took off. It was a pitchout, and Borker gave it a good try. But he didn't have the arm. His throw arched, and by the time Davey Lundgren had it, Flagg had slid in and come right up in one motion, like a major leaguer. These kids were real athletes and they were well coached too.

"Here we go," Mr. Stevens muttered. We were being stampeded by a bunch of wild horses.

"Forget about him, Steve," Ollie called out, "that's as far as this guy goes."

Ollie made a feinting move to his left to force Flagg back. He was taking an enormous lead off second. Flagg didn't move. He stood there, hands on hips, taunting Steve. Steve stepped off the rubber and Flagg ran back to second. The Hardwares bench erupted in a series of insults at Steve telling him to either throw the ball or go play the outfield.

"You ain't gonna win a game steppin' off the rubber, man," someone on their bench yelled.

It was the truth, too, I thought.

"Work on the batter, Steve," Mr. Stevens called out.

"Flagg'll go down," I said.

"I know he will," Mr. Stevens said.

Turner threw to the plate. Flagg, with his enormous lead, took off for third. He was there before the ball even reached the plate. I guess the batter really liked what he saw because he stepped into the pitch and smashed a sizzling liner right at Steve. Steve did the only sensible thing, he ducked.

The Hardwares yelled, and then we yelled right back, for coming out of nowhere, running full tilt, arm outstretched, Ollie made a sensational catch and stepped on second for an easy double play.

Out of disaster we'd plucked profit.

Tommy Flagg stood at third in disbelief. "You guys," he said softly, "are luck-ee."

"And it's about time, too," Mr. Stevens muttered. "Way to go, Ollie."

"Good catch, Ollie."

"Way to snag them, big man."

It was a fielding gem, the kind that picks you right up and makes you feel so good. Our guys were talking it up. Thirty seconds after the play was over, our parents were still clapping.

For a game we were supposed to lose, we were not lying down. And I had the feeling something different was going to happen. But a lot depended on how we batted against Malkus, who was now stepping up to the plate—he was their number three hitter.

Lonnie had a stiff way of swinging the bat before the pitch came—swinging it downward, not breaking his wrists at all the way you're supposed to. But I guess it was a rhythm thing with him because when a pitch he liked came in, he could swing and break his wrists all right. He swung viciously and with power.

Instinctively, our outfielders backed up. Lonnie looked intimidating at the plate.

Steve seemed restored to confidence out there. There is nothing like a double play to make a pitcher feel relaxed. He starts believing in the team behind him and that means he can throw all kinds of pitches. He doesn't have to strike out a guy to get an out, and usually that is when you can strike people out. Steve was pitching with empty bags, and Lonnie did present a big target area.

Steve pumped and threw. He put his whole body behind the pitch. It sailed over Lonnie's head. The ball rolled to the backstop and brought on a chorus of jeers from the Hardwares bench.

"He ain't that big, Turner."

"Get a ladder, Lonnie."

"Do your thing, man."

Lonnie's thing was to hit it. Steve's next pitch was high, too, but Lonnie, anxious to give it a whack, reached up and hit it. He sent a towering fly ball to center field. Ray Panello was under it. He pounded his glove twice and caught it, and our guys came running in, talking it up. This was the first time we hadn't been scored on in the first inning by the Hardwares. But we were lucky—Ollie's great catch, and then Lonnie too eager, had bailed us out. If Lonnie had waited for a pitch at shoulder level or below, he wouldn't have hit under the pitch.

It was funny how much more I saw knowing I didn't have to play. It was really enjoyable watching baseball's little things. Uncle Ned and Dad were always saying baseball was an art, made up of little things that people often missed. I'd missed them because I was so worried about doing poorly on the diamond. Now I was more a part of this game out of it than I used to be in it.

Mr. Stevens slapped all the guys on the back as they came in. He was awfully up, I thought, for a game we couldn't win.

"Now let's give these guys a taste of their own medicine," he said. "Lundgren, Brown, Stevens, Felch. Randy, get out there and pep these guys up."

I went out to the third base coaching box, in street clothes and with Mr. Stevens's cap on my head. I felt a little self-conscious, aware that our parents were looking at me, smiling, and Junior Russell was also giving me a sideways look.

"Hey, man, where's your coach?"

"I'm coaching today."

"Yeah. I sees that. But how come you ain't playing?"

"I got hurt a while back."

"Yeah. I know you. You saved Sam Gonder."

"You know him?"

"Yeah. Everyone knows him."

"Tell him Randy says hello."

"C'mon, Junior," the Hardwares coach called out, "you here to talk or play baseball?"

"Play ball, man," Junior said, winked at me, spat in his glove, shuffled his feet, and called out to Lonnie. "Let's go get 'em, big man."

I watched Junior move down the line toward home. He was pretty sure no one could get around on Lonnie's fast ball. I looked over to the first baseman who was big and didn't look too fast. He was playing level with his bag.

Davey Lundgren looked at me for a signal. I touched one elbow, then the other elbow, and then casually took my cap off. It might be nice to try to stampede the Hardwares. Davey looked casually at Junior playing way in, but I nodded vaguely across the diamond and he got the point without looking.

"Batter up," the ump said.

Davey stepped in.

Do it on the first pitch, Davey, I thought, let's terrorize *them*.

"Hey, Batter, I feel wild today," Lonnie Malkus called out, grinning.

"Shut up and pitch, Malkus," Ollie said.

Lonnie pumped and came down. Davey squared around to bunt down the first base line. But the pitch was too hot to handle. It slithered foul off the end of his bat. I noticed that the first baseman did not come charging in. He was expecting either the pitcher or catcher to handle it.

File it away. I remember Dad saying that memory was

one of a ball player's best tools. What a guy did on a certain kind of batted ball . . . or bunted ball.

"He gonna bunt on Joe Bibbs. That's what he thought he'd do."

"They ain't got no hitter. They don't even got bunters."

Davey looked down at me. The first baseman had moved in a little. Junior at third was in. I signaled Davey to hit away.

He tried to, but the fast ball was again too much. It was high and Davey went fishing.

The Hardwares jeered him.

Davey stepped out of the box and rubbed some dirt on his hands. No balls and two strikes. He wasn't going to look down at me; he knew he had to protect the plate.

The first baseman had backed up.

I took my cap off. "Davey," I called. He looked at me, at my bare head, blinked, as he tried to figure out what I wanted. Finally he realized I was trying to tell him to bunt with two strikes on him. It was his only chance to get on. They would not be expecting a bunt.

He stepped in. "Be tough up there, Dave," I shouted. "It only takes one to do it."

No one in their right mind bunts with two strikes on them, especially against a fast ball pitcher.

"All them signals ain't gonna help you, Davey," Lonnie Malkus called out to him.

"He was signaling for him to duck," Tommy Flagg called out from shortstop.

Lonnie reared back and threw another fast ball. Davey

bunted it fair down the first base line. It caught the catcher and first baseman napping. Lonnie finally ran over and picked it up, but Davey was across first base by then.

A roar went up from our bench. Mr. Stevens's eyebrows shot up, but then he decided to clap his hands, too. It wasn't orthodox baseball, but it had worked.

I decided to press our luck. To try and do to the Hardwares what they did to everyone else. Pour it on, hard and early. I gave Davey the steal signal, made sure Doodie saw it. I wanted Doodie protecting him when he went down.

It was a risky thing to do. No one stole much on Joe Bibbs, the catcher. He had the arm of a fifteen-year-old kid, and we were still playing on sixty-foot diamonds. But I figured we might catch them napping. With a two-strike bunter safe on first, they might think we'd settle for little things.

Lonnie muttered dark incomprehensible words to Doodie and fired away. Davey took off. The ball was in the dirt. Bibbs knocked it down and held onto it. Davey hook slid into second.

Our bench was alive now. No one, but no one, took such liberties with the Belden Hardwares.

Bibbs fired the ball back at Lonnie. "C'mon, man," he said.

"That bunt was yours," Lonnie fired back at him. He was still angry about the previous play. If we could get Malkus to lose his temper. . . .

Tommy Flagg came in from shortstop to calm Lonnie

down. None of us had ever seen the big pitcher rattled before and it was fun to see.

I took advantage of the time out to call Doodie out of the batter's box. We huddled halfway. And Doodie right then and there paid me the biggest compliment anyone on the team ever had. He said: "What do you want me to do, Randy?"

"Lay it down on the second pitch. Towards first. We might as well bother the first baseman while we're at it."

"Gotcha."

Their conference broke up and so did ours. I kept my eye on Flagg as he walked back to shortstop. I remember Dad telling a story once how a hidden ball trick was prepared while the third base coach was talking with the batter.

But Flagg didn't have the ball; it was in Lonnie's hand. My cap was off when Davey looked at me. He nodded. I put it on and went through a lot of meaningless signals.

Davey took a big lead as Lonnie went to a stretch. Flagg cut for the bag. Lonnie whirled to throw to second and Davey, acting on instincts you have to be born with, took off for third. Already committed to his throw to second, Lonnie tried to check it and ended up throwing the ball in the dirt. Davey took a big turn at third. I held him up.

"Way to go, Davey."

Our guys started razzing Lonnie. "Hey, Malkus, what kind of pitch was that?"

"That's his dirt pitch."

"Who's on first, Lonnie?"

"They're falling apart, gang."

The Hardwares coach called time and went out to talk to his team. He knew what was happening, that we were trying to do to them what they did to everyone else, gallop away with the game in the early innings. I could hear him telling them to settle down, to forget about the runner on third, to play for the sure out at first. They'd get a dozen runs before this game was over.

Meanwhile, Davey and I talked quietly. "What do you think, Randy?"

"Play it safe. Go down the line if he winds up. But it's not worth going all the way now. We got three guys who can drive you in."

The ump broke up the Hardwares' meeting. Lonnie was still kicking at the dirt, which meant he was mad at himself. Dad always says you got a game half won when the other pitcher is mad at himself. Pitching is 90 percent concentration on a batter's weakness, and when a pitcher's mad at himself, he can't see a thing.

It was one ball and no strikes on Doodie. I kept my cap on, gave him no signs, and told him to hit away. Lonnie went to a full windup. Davey went down the line. The pitch came in and to everyone's surprise, mine too, Doodie bunted. A little squib in front of the plate. Joe Bibbs pounced on it and braced himself for the collision at home. He thought it was a squeeze play. But there was no squeeze. Davey was scampering back to third while Doodie was hotfooting it across the bag at first.

You would have thought the championship was ours. Our parents, who hadn't expected to have anything to cheer about, started hollering as though they were at a football game. Our bench was hollering, and best of all Lonnie and Joe Bibbs were arguing about that last play.

Their coach told them to cut it out and play baseball, but Lonnie was finished. He walked Ollie on four straight pitches, and their coach came out and brought in Tommy Flagg to pitch. Lonnie went out to shortstop. Two bunt singles, a walk, and some clever baserunning had rid us of one of the best pitchers in the eleven-year-old league.

For a while, anyway. He was still in the game, and their coach could bring him back any time he wanted.

But for now it would be a relief to bat against Tommy Flagg. He was a tough cool kid who pitched like Davey Lundgren did. Control, courage, and good fielding. But he threw balls you could hit, and Jimmy Felch, our cleanup hitter, stepped into Flagg's first pitch and belted a home run between left and center. A grand slam homer. I was so busy waving guys around third base I thought my arm would fall off.

After that Otto hit the ball, Panello hit the ball, Turner and Borker hit the ball. Everyone was hitting. We got two more runs before the inning was over.

"Who says we can't win on this diamond?" Jim Felch asked.

The diamond didn't seem uphill anymore, the wind was blowing for us, and the sun was shining in *their* eyes.

We were beating the Hardwares 6-0 in the top of the second and who would have believed a thing like that?

When I went back to the bench, Mr. Stevens shook my hand solemnly. "Some nifty coaching out there, Randy."

He didn't say it, but I knew he was puzzled as to how a kid who hated playing baseball could know so much about the game. But he didn't know about those endless hours of baseball talk between Dad and Uncle Ned and Teddy and his older brothers that I used to sit and listen to. I never thought it would pay off, though.

Well, the fact is, it didn't quite pay off, for what started off so wonderfully ended up quite badly, and the coach who was the hero of the first inning, I am sorry to report to you, turned out to be the goat of the last.

9 · DISASTER STRIKES

EVEN IN OUR nutty league, a 6-0 lead should be enough to win. But I guess we just weren't used to big leads or something because after the second inning we stopped hustling and started protecting, sitting on our lead. And that's always a mistake. You give the other team a chance to get started.

In the top of the second, Steve Turner got them out in order, but the way he did it was scary. Each of their three batters hit the ball solidly, but right at someone. Ollie grabbed a liner at short, Jim Felch caught a shot in deep left, and Doodie made a good play on a ground ball, throwing Junior Russell out by a half-step.

It didn't look good. One of these innings their balls would have eyes on them and find the holes between fielders.

When I went out to coach in the bottom of the second, Junior Russell looked over at me. "You guys are lucky today. But we gonna get you."

"Not a chance," I replied.

We didn't get any more runs in the bottom of the second, and in the top of the third their number seven batter, the second baseman, hit a ground ball that was all eyes. It found a hole between Ollie and Doodie and sneaked through into left field.

Steve didn't look bothered, but I thought he was tiring a little. Not because he was throwing too many pitches—he wasn't—but because he was bearing down, concentrating on each pitch. Emotion can drain you fast.

Now there was a runner on first to worry about, and like all the Hardwares he was fast. He took a big leadoff and began taunting Steve. Steve threw over to Otto, not seriously, but just to let the kid know he could do it. Steve next tried to "look him back" toward first, but the kid wasn't having any. "C'mon, Pitcher," he said, "git me out, if you can."

Steve threw to the plate, and the kid took off. He made second easily. Was this going to be a replay of the first inning? I hoped so—but the next batter hit an outside pitch between Otto and Davey, and the Hardwares had their first run.

We told Steve not to worry, just to chuck away, but Steve was worrying plenty now. Trying to pitch to cor-ners, he began aiming the ball and missing the strike zone. He walked the next man.

Mr. Stevens looked at me. "Who would you pitch, Randy? Ollie or Lundgren?"

It was a good question. We had to win either this game or the next one to get a good berth in the playoffs. We were supposed to be saving Ollie for Baer Machine—the game we had a chance to win. But we now had a five-run lead in a game we were supposed to lose. A bird in the hand is worth two in the bush. Better, I thought, to go all out in this one. Pitch Ollie now, even though if he pitched the rest of the game he'd only have two innings of eligibility left against Baer Machine.

A five-run lead was still a lot of lead. Let's protect it. I told Mr. Stevens what I thought.

He said we'd see what Steve did with the next batter.

Steve didn't do much with him. He walked him in five pitches. He was straining now, reaching back too far when he threw. That lead was going to dissolve very fast. They'd crack Steve open so fast now. . . .

"Time, Ump," Mr. Stevens called, and went out to the mound. The whole infield grouped around them. The Hardwares, sensing the kill, were noising it up. When Mr. Stevens brought in Ollie to pitch, they really cheered. They knew Ollie. They knew he was our best pitcher. They were the kind of kids who liked to beat you with their best against your best. They'd beaten Ollie earlier this season. They weren't afraid of him; they weren't afraid of anyone.

Davey Lundgren moved to short; Steve went to second. While Ollie warmed up, Otto fed them ground balls. Mr. Stevens sat down alongside me.

"Keep your fingers crossed."

"My toes too."

Kerplunk! Ollie's fast ball slammed into Borker's big mitt.

"Man, he's a swift one."

"Hey, Ollie, go easy on us poor kids."

"Watch out you don't balk, Ollie. You got the bases loaded."

"Hey, Flagg, watch out for that fast one of his."

Tommy Flagg, swinging two bats, grinned and spat about ten feet. I always wondered why the best ball players were also the best spitters.

Borker threw the last warm-up pitch back to Ollie.

"Talk it up, boys," Mr. Stevens called out.

The infield started chattering, quietly, because they were a little nervous now.

"Just chuck away, Ollie," Mr. Stevens said. "Just fire them in there."

That's what Ollie did best. He fired away. He wasn't a canny pitcher. He was really a shortstop with a great arm, and in our league that was usually good enough. He also never got a case of the nerves. If it wasn't a great hitting team he was facing, Ollie could usually get them out. He had a good rising fast ball, and a change-of-pace pitch that was very effective.

Tommy Flagg stepped in, swinging with a choked bat. Ollie ignored the runner on third and went to a full windup. The runner went down the line yelling: "Here I come. Here I come."

Ollie's pitch was low, but Flagg swung and slapped a grounder at Doodie. It was an easy play at the plate. Doodie should have had it, but the ball skidded under his glove and into left field. Two runs scored and only good fielding by Jimmy Felch kept Flagg on first. They had men on first and third now. The score was 6-3, and I could feel the bottom falling out.

"C'mon, guys," I shouted, "let's not give them any more."

Doodie was mad at himself. He was kicking the dirt. Once a guy as good as Doodie makes an error, there's the danger of other guys making errors. It's like catching a cold.

With men on first and third, we had to think what to do. Mr. Stevens cupped his hands over his mouth. "You got runners on first and third, boys, what're you gonna do?"

He was reminding them that Flagg would surely be trying to steal second, and if our catcher threw down to second, then the kid on third would surely go home. Every team in our league worked this double steal unless they had a very slow runner on third. No one on the Hardwares was slow.

But just as every team worked this double steal, so every team had a play to counteract it. It was very simple. When the guy on first took off for second, the second baseman yelled: "He's coming." The catcher stood up and fired the ball over the middle. The pitcher caught it and fired it right back to nail the runner coming home. The trouble was it never worked because everyone knew what everyone else was doing, so the runner on third never moved until he saw the throw really going to second.

Ollie and Mark Borker double-checked signals and finally Ollie was ready. He threw to the plate. Flagg sprinted to second. Mark fired it toward there. Ollie grabbed it and fired it right back at Mark. It was all pretty silly because the runner on third had run back to third and he was standing there with a big grin on his face.

None out, Hardwares on second and third, the tying run was at the plate. Mr. Stevens signaled the infield to play in.

It would be hard getting anyone out at the plate, I thought. It would have to be a perfectly hit grounder, a perfect throw to Borker, and Borker would have to put the tag on a hard-sliding Hardware.

Still, it was the right idea. And when their number two batter smacked a hard grounder down the third base line, I thought we had them. Doodie moved beautifully, grabbed the ball, and in one motion fired to Mark. Mark had it. The runner slid. Mark put the tag on him but at the last second the kid kicked his left foot up and he kicked the ball out of Mark's hand. It was unfair, but legal.

"Safe," the ump called.

"Mark," Doodie screamed. Mark pounced on the ball and threw it to third, but Flagg was in safe in a swirl of dust, and their other runner took off for second. Doodie faked a throw to second and held on. Flagg lay there, safe on the bag, grinning up at him. The stampede was on. Ollie was upset. He should have had two outs by now. Instead they had scored two more runs and our lead was getting smaller, 6-4.

"That's all right, Ollie," Mr. Stevens called out. "You're doing fine. Just keep firing."

"Shouldn't we put Lonnie on and try for a force at the plate?" I asked.

It meant putting the winning run on base but we'd have a better chance of cutting a run off at the plate if we didn't have to tag someone. Besides, Lonnie was a tremendous hitter.

Mr. Stevens nodded. He called time and went out and talked to Mark and Ollie. When he came back, he was smiling grimly. "They told me they were going to do it anyway." He patted my shoulder. "Well, we're all thinking alike even if we're booting a few."

The Hardwares booed Ollie as he pitched four wide ones and put Lonnie on, loading up the bases.

Up stepped Joe Bibbs, their cleanup hitter. I didn't think he hit as consistently as Lonnie. Ollie walked around the mound, checking his outfield, waving Jimmy over toward the line. Bases loaded, nobody out, our fans were silent, nervous. So were we. Only Mr. Stevens and I were talking it up for our side.

"Fire away, Ollie," he said.

"Play at home," I said.

Ollie looked in for his signal, which was not a real one. He would go with only one pitch now—his fast ball—but Mr. Stevens insisted on signals in order to slow a pitcher down and give him a rhythm. Ollie went to a full windup. Flagg went down the line. Bibbs swung and smacked the ball right back at Ollie. It almost took his head off. Steve dove for it at second, but he didn't have a chance. Ray Panello came in fast, trying to scoop it up and throw home in one motion the way major leaguers do on TV. Well, it may work on the tube but in real life it goes under your glove and all the way out to the tall grass in center field where you look for it, your heart and head pounding, hearing the shouts and yells and knowing you've done a stupid thing, given the Hardwares a grand slam home run. Four runs. The score was now 8-6.

Ollie stood at the mound, his face pale.

Mr. Stevens wanted to go out and talk to him but a second trip out would mean he'd have to take Ollie off the mound so he walked up to the foul line and called out to him: "That was a lucky hit. We'll get it back. Come on, Ollie, be tough. Fight back."

But Mr. Stevens could shout encouragement all he wanted, our guys were still in a state of shock. A 6-0 lead had vanished. We were now behind. The Hardwares were laughing, yelling, pounding their bats against the ground. Ollie stomped around angrily. That was the first clean hit off him, and it should have been held to a single. Out in center field Ray Panello stood there, head down. I knew what he was feeling. He was looking for that rock to crawl under.

Only Davey Lundgren seemed OK. "C'mon, guys," he said, and blew a bubble of gum, "we can get it back. Let's get these guys out."

His voice was flat and reassuring. Ollie nodded. He glanced at Ray Panello out in center. Ray nodded, and moved back.

Then Ollie started pitching. He threw as hard as I'd

ever seen him throw. He just fired the fast ball in there. The next batter popped it up to Doodie. He struck out the next two guys, one of them Junior Russell whose batting average had to be way below a thousand now.

But the damage was done. The question now was: do we concede the game and take Ollie out and let Steve or Dave Lundgren pitch the last three innings, giving Ollie five innings of eligibility for Baer Machine, or do we play to win?

Mr. Stevens decided to play to win. I agreed with him. There was nothing so bad for team morale as giving up. Also, if you had it in you to give up in one situation, you had it in you to give up in all situations. I remember Dad saying this one night.

In the bottom of the third we hit Tommy Flagg hard, but we didn't get any runs out of it. They never really hit Ollie again. He was firing and our guys had settled down and were fielding cleanly. In the sixth and last inning of regulation play, the score was still 8-6 in their favor. And we had our confidence back. After all, we had shown it was possible to score six runs in one inning against the great Hardwares. Just half that total would give us the win.

In the top of the sixth, with his fast ball clipping along, Ollie struck out Flagg, got their number two man on a pop-up to Otto. Lonnie belted a double into left center, but Joe Bibbs flied out to Ray Panello, and we came running in for our last licks.

"We can do it, guys," I said.

"Everybody hits."

"Ray gets on and he goes all the way."

"Panello, Turner, Borker, Palwicz. . . ." Mr. Stevens read off. It was the tail end of the lineup, but these guys who swung with choked bats could hit Flagg as well as the top end.

Panello was a good man to lead off. He was the fastest runner on the team. Not the best base stealer, but he had the most "track" speed. He was a slightly built dark-haired boy who could really fly once he got started.

While he swung a bat with the lead doughnut, I told him I thought he ought to bunt. But as he stepped into the batter's box, Junior Russell came way in, and so did the first baseman. All great minds run alike. I just yelled down to Ray: "Bunt's off. Hit away."

The Hardwares thought I was kidding. They didn't move back. But Ray knew I wasn't kidding. He took a high pitch for a ball and didn't square around.

Junior Russell turned around to me. "Is he gonna bunt or not, Randy?"

"He won't bunt, Junior. You better move back."

Junior grinned and moved in a little closer. He had figured what a Hardware would say to a question like that. Flagg pitched and Ray slapped a ground ball right at Junior. An easy grounder if Junior weren't just twenty feet away, but it bounced off Junior's shins and rolled off the field. Junior hobbled after it. Ray took a big turn. Junior threw the ball to second and Ray went back to first.

"Oooh, ooh," Junior said, walking around gingerly.

We razzed him. His own team razzed him.

"I told you," I said.

He gave me a hurt look. "I thought you was fooling me," he said.

While Junior walked around in pain, Joe Bibbs and Flagg were talking it over. I also heard their second baseman telling Lonnie at short that he, the second baseman, would cover second on a steal because the batter was right-handed. Those were team players, I thought; they looked after each other.

The meeting over, Junior's shins feeling better, Bibbs squatted down and gave his signal. Flagg went to his set position, and then threw over to first. Ray was back easily. He didn't take big leads. He wasn't quick; he was fast. He knew he didn't have the baseball instincts of a Lundgren or an Ollie, so he sensibly didn't take any chances. Once he got moving, though, and thought out what he should do, he could almost outrace a ball.

Flagg set, and then pitched. Ray took off for second. Steve Turner chopped at the ball, hoping to bother Bibbs. But no one bothered Bibbs. The big catcher caught the ball and fired down to second base. His throw had Ray beat, but the second baseman started to put the tag on Ray before he had the ball, and it went through his glove. Lonnie Malkus, who should have been backing up the play, was standing there at shortstop watching the action.

Ray slid in, looked at the ball bouncing into center field, and then looked at me for a signal.

"Come on," I screamed. "Run."

He hesitated, and then got up and ran toward third. We'd never have another opportunity like this, I thought. But I was wrong. We didn't have a chance then.

Their center fielder came out of nowhere. Running

hard, he picked up the ball with his bare hand and fired it on one bounce to Junior Russell at third.

Junior had the ball as Ray arrived. Ray was thin; Junior was solid. Ray was flying off balance, not knowing whether to slide or not. It was too late to slide. Junior's feet were planted. Ray tried to twist around him. Junior slammed his glove with the ball in it against Ray's left hip. Ray went down hard . . . and just lay there.

"Out," the bases ump called and jerked his thumb skyward.

Out cold, he should have said. Ray wasn't moving. Mr. Stevens was off the bench and running. I just stood there, paralyzed, looking down at Ray. Why had I waved him on? I was responsible for this. I felt sick.

"Ray," Mr. Stevens said, "look at me."

Ray looked at him. Then he winced and cried out.

"Where does it hurt?"

"My . . . leg."

"Here?"

"Yes, ooh. . . ." Tears were in Ray's eyes.

"We better get him to the hospital. It might be a muscle or a ligament. . . ."

The Hardwares coach bent over Ray. "Does it hurt when you move it or all the time?"

"All . . . the time."

"He may have busted something in there."

"Ed," Mr. Stevens said, "ask your father to come over here, will you?"

Ed Palwicz got his father and Mr. Borker, too. Together they made a chair lift of their hands and carried Ray over to the Palwicz car. I walked with them. Ray was

110

in terrific pain. They put him in the car and both men drove him off to the hospital.

When I got back to my coaching box there was Junior Russell apologizing to anyone who would listen to him. Mr. Stevens reassured him. "You didn't do anything, Junior. You made the right play. He was late coming down; he should have slid. You always slide on a close play."

Mr. Stevens didn't say anything to me.

"There goes the ball game," someone said.

"The Baer Machine game, too."

"And the playoffs."

They didn't say a thing to me about my signaling Ray to come down. In a way that hurt more than anything.

Mr. Stevens clapped his hands. "C'mon, boys, dobbers up. This game isn't over yet."

But it was. Borker and Ed Palwicz went down like lambs.

When it was over we just sat there in shock. A six-run lead blown. Our best pitcher wasted. Our center fielder in the hospital.

"Randy, pack up the equipment bag," Mr. Stevens said.

I packed the bag and hoisted it on my shoulder. The bat handles dug into my flesh, but I carried it alone without stopping, all the way. I'd blown the game for the Bakers with my call at third. I'd blown the playoffs, and the season. Worst of all, I'd put one of my teammates in the hospital.

Baseball was a lousy game.

The Buhr diamond was a lousy diamond.

I stumbled across it with the equipment bag.

10 · NON-INSTANT REPLAY

AFTER SUPPER, WHICH was late because of my game, I
went outside and "fished the garden." In successive casts,
I laid the end of my line in the rose bushes, by the honey-
suckle, by the vines from our neighbor's yard which tried
to choke our apple tree.

I fished by the light of the dining-room chandelier. The
windows were open and they were still seated at the
table: Mom, Dad, Nan, Julie, Mary, and Uncle Ned and
Aunt Ruthie who'd come over for dessert. I was plenty
glad they hadn't brought Teddy along because he would
have wanted to know all the gory details of our defeat.

As it was, I just told them we lost and started eating.

Dad was curious and would have wanted details but luckily Mary began yammering on her latest favorite subject —the Michigammes, a girls' track team that was being formed down at Ferry Field. Girls her age were in it, running five miles a day, and she wanted to join. Nan called her a "jockette," Julie said it would make her calves too big, and Mom said she simply didn't have time to drive her to Ferry Field every day. Dad didn't say a thing. I knew he was waiting for Uncle Ned to have an opinion.

Uncle Ned laughed. "It's a big thing around the country these days. Girls' track teams."

"I think Mary's too young," Aunt Ruthie said.

"If you get big calves, the boys won't like you," Julie said, teasing her.

"I don't like boys," Mary said. "I wanna run."

"Wait a few years, Mary," Uncle Ned said. "You start competing at the age of ten, at fifteen you'll be sick of it. That's one of the problems with this Little League business, I think. Too much pressure too early."

"I don't agree," Dad said. "A kid learns to take pressure."

"*Some* kids," Uncle Ned said. "Other kids have to grow into it."

And then they started arguing. Dad always argued with Uncle Ned. Whenever they were together, he was a younger brother. While they argued about the right age for a kid to start competing in athletics, I slipped out the back door and fished quietly. I fished the compost heap and the forsythia bush and wondered if this family of mine could ever talk about anything else but athletics.

The phone rang and I watched Mom walk out of the

dining room and into the kitchen to answer it. Then I heard the back screen door open.

"Randy, are you out there?"

"Yes, Ma."

"It's for you. It's Mr. Stevens."

I just stood there.

"Randy, did you hear me? It's Mr. Stevens."

I froze because I knew what it was going to be. I guess part of me had known from the moment the two fathers had taken Ray off in the car to the hospital.

"Randy, are you going to answer the phone or should I tell him you're sick?"

"I'm coming. . . ."

My mother gave me a strange look. I picked up the phone. "Hello, Mr. Stevens."

"Randy, how are you? All recovered? Good. Look, I know it was pretty bad today. But we'll bounce back. We have to. We're going to beat Baer Machine and twenty Bob Skaneckis. If we can get six runs in one inning off the Hardwares, we can get twenty off Baer Machine. But I've got some bad news. Ray is finished for the season. He's got a hairline fracture of his ankle. He's in a cast already. I'm afraid you're our number nine man. I've called the Wrights, but there's no answer, so I guess they're not back from vacation yet. We can start a game with eight men, but we can't play past the second inning without a ninth man. So you've got to suit up again. Randy, you still have your uniform, don't you? Good. Now, don't sound so sad. You showed me a different Randy McElroy on the bench. A Randy that talked it up, that knew a lot about baseball. I know you can transfer that knowledge into action. I'm going to play you either in right or at second, depending on who I pitch against Baer Machine. If I start Davey, you'll be at second. If I start Steve, you'll be in right. Ollie's got two innings of eligibility left, I'm going to save him for the end. The game's at Vets, Thursday, at 5:45. Will you need a ride? No, OK, I'd like to see you there a half hour early, at 5:15. Listen, Randy, you haven't swung a bat in a while. It might be a good idea to find someone to throw a few balls to you. I know if *I'd* been out of baseball all summer, that's what I'd do. But you decide for yourself. . . ."

And on he went. I half-listened to him. It was back to baseball. The end of the happy summer. And I'd done it to myself.

"So . . . we'll see you in uniform, won't we?"

"Yes, Mr. Stevens."

He hung up. I stood there a moment and then started toward the back door again. Mom spoke to me from the dining room. "What did Mr. Stevens want, Randy?"

"He's Randy's coach," Dad explained to Uncle Ned.

"Coach? I thought Randy had quit baseball."

"He's scorekeeping for his team. I guess they lost a tough one today. What was the score, Randy?"

"Eight-six." I opened the back door.

"Come in here, Randy," Mom said. "I don't care for conversations that go from one room to another."

Reluctantly, I went back in the dining room. Nan smiled at me. "How was the fishing out there?"

"Not so good."

Nan turned to Aunt Ruthie. "Randy once caught our neighbor's beech tree."

115

"Is that right? What did you do with it, Randy."

"Threw it back."

Uncle Ned laughed. "There's no limit on beeches, is there?"

"No," I smiled.

"What did Mr. Stevens want?" Dad asked.

I took a deep breath. "He wanted to tell me that I'd have to play in the last regular season game."

The silence that greeted this was awesome.

"Who's going on vacation?" Julie asked.

"No one. Ray Panello got hurt."

"Oh, dear," Mom said. "What happened to him?"

"He fractured his leg."

"Today?"

"Yes."

"Oh, that's awful."

"How did it happen, Randy?" Dad asked.

So now it had to come out. They'd find out sooner or later. It was probably better that they find out from me. So with all of them looking at me, and me feeling like I was on stage, I told them about the whole business. How Mr. Stevens let me coach at third. How we got off to a 6-0 lead and then blew it. How I'd yelled to Ray to come on, how if I hadn't yelled he wouldn't have busted his leg and I wouldn't have to be putting on a baseball uniform again. I had messed things up coaching and now I was going to mess things up playing. We were sure to lose to Baer Machine if I played. I'd give my right arm to be able to relive that moment at third when Ray looked at me to tell him what to do and I . . .

When I was done, nobody said a thing. I guess they

116

were all embarrassed that I could screw things up and not even be in the lineup.

Uncle Ned looked puzzled. "Randy, tell me something. Was the shortstop backing up the second baseman when the ball went through his legs?"

"No. He was standing there watching."

"Did your runner . . . what's his name?"

"Ray."

"Did Ray see what was happening?"

"He must have. He slid in looking that way."

"Then what did he do?"

"He looked at me for a signal. I told him to keep coming. I didn't see the center fielder running in."

Uncle Ned smiled. "You didn't see him running in because he wasn't in the picture at that moment. More time went by than you knew. What happened wasn't all your fault, Randy. In a play like that the runner is on his own. He's his own best judge of what to do. He's got the vision and he knows how good his legs are at any given moment. He should have got right up and headed for third. But he decided to look to you to tell him what to do. He wasted the time, not you. Your coaching move was the correct one, maybe a little late, but it was late because of him, not you. The fact is, you shouldn't have had to make that signal in the first place. Mr. Stevens should have chewed out the runner, not you."

"He didn't chew me out, Uncle Ned. No one did. I sort of wished they had. No one said a thing to me."

"Randy, they didn't chew you out because it wasn't your fault. And they couldn't chew Ray out because you don't chew out kids with broken legs."

Dad laughed. "Do you remember the time you yelled at Gus Manakos for not getting up after his shoestring catch against East Lansing?"

Uncle Ned blushed. "Gus broke his arm making that catch," he explained to everyone.

"And when he showed Ned a busted arm, Ned told him he should have thrown it with his left arm. Ned told him he blew an easy double play."

"I was young then," Uncle Ned said, and he was blushing so hard we all laughed.

I felt better. Better because I really believed they weren't just trying to make me feel better, but were truly analyzing what had happened.

"What about your playing now?" Dad asked. "You haven't swung a bat in quite a while."

"Dad, practice isn't going to help me."

"Well, can *I* see you swing a bat, Randy?" Uncle Ned asked.

"It's too dark outside, Ned," Aunt Ruthie said.

"No, I mean here. In the house. In the living room."

"Nobody is going to swing a bat in my living room," Mom said.

"Randy never hits anything," Julie said.

That *was* funny, and I laughed too. Mary, businesslike, went to the athletic box and brought back a bat.

"Go into the living room and swing it," Uncle Ned said. "I can see you from here."

"Wait a minute," Mom said. "I'm going to move the standing lamp. And you be careful you don't hit anything else."

She unplugged the lamp and put it against the fire-place. "Be careful, Randy."

"OK," Uncle Ned said.

I swung easy. It felt funny in the living room.

"Swing harder."

"This is making me nervous," Mom said.

"Go ahead," Dad said.

I swung hard.

"That's enough," Mom said. "I don't like this game. Put the bat away. I'm glad we've got the front curtains drawn. Anyone looking in would think this family is nuts."

"They are."

"Well?" Dad asked.

"You want my analysis," Uncle Ned said solemnly. "It's this: Randy is going to make one heckuva football player."

Laughter. "I knew he'd say that," Aunt Ruthie said. "Don't feel bad, Randy."

"I don't."

"Do you remember, big brother, the time I put a cross block on you when the junior varsity played the varsity your senior year?"

"You never put a block on me in your life, Jack."

"Oh, didn't I? I can remember who was carrying the ball and where you were. It was. . . ."

They started remembering a football play that took place more than twenty years ago. I listened for a few minutes and then when nobody was paying any attention I slipped out the back door and picked up my fishing rod.

I whipped the line back and forth in memory of the happy summer . . . which was now all over.

119

11 · RETURN TO
THE BASEBALL WARS

ALL DAY WEDNESDAY I was nervous. I tried to cure my nervousness at the river, but even that old medicine didn't work. I tried casting for the old bullhead, but no luck. I didn't even see him once.

Mrs. Gonder and I talked about finding new places to fish west of town but she didn't have a car and we agreed the fishing was probably bad all over.

Finally, I gave up and went home. Mom got me to cut our grass and when I was done she asked me to go around the block and cut Mrs. Payson's grass. Cutting Mrs. Payson's grass was a McElroy tradition. Mrs. Payson was an old widow lady who lived alone in a small house with a lot of lawn. Teddy cuts her grass, his older brothers used to cut her grass, and I even think my father, when he was a kid, used to cut her grass. She was a nice old lady who'd talk your ear off, pay you fifty cents for two hours' work, and give you dry cookies that made you thirsty. Her lawn was hard too. It had ups and downs in it. And she wanted all the grass clippings collected on the street and the sidewalk brushed off. And after you were done, she gave you the two quarters and the cookies, and called you Ted. She thought I was my cousin, and I didn't put her straight figuring she'd call on Teddy next time for the lawn.

But it was good for my nerves because I didn't think about tomorrow's game at all and I got good and tired. I went to bed real early but I was so tired I couldn't sleep. I lay in bed and listened to the cicada and remembered reading an article about seventeen-year cicada and how they lived underground for seventeen years sucking sap from tree roots and then emerged, flew around for two months, laid eggs, and died. I felt a little like a cicada holed up for all of a Michigan winter, released for a couple of summer months to do what? Play baseball . . . and die. I'd lay my eggs at the plate tomorrow. Ray Panello, I could kill you. Why didn't you run when you should have? Why didn't you have the brains to ignore me when you should have?

The next day it rained. It rained all day, and my return to the baseball wars was postponed to Saturday morning. We heard the news on one of the local radio stations.

121

That's how the league notifies teams that their games are canceled. On a rainy day you're supposed to listen to the radio all day.

Ollie called to tell me the game was postponed till Saturday morning at Vets Park at 10 A.M.

I asked him if anyone would be back from vacation by then.

"No," he said gloomily.

"There's no chance Ray's leg will be better by Saturday. . . ."

"Aw, Randy, quit dreaming."

The postponement till Saturday would give my uncle Ned a chance to see me play. He told me over the phone he'd be coming down with Dad.

"It's going to be a terrible game," I said.

"Don't worry," he said, "you won't hear a peep out of me."

My cousin Teddy threatened to come, too, unless I bought him a Dairy Queen, so we biked over and I bought him a Dairy Queen.

The postponement till Saturday gave me that much more time to get nervous, but strangely, I didn't. I guess a guy has only got so much nervousness in him. Friday night I slept the best I had all summer. I was just plain exhausted.

Saturday morning was beautiful. A perfect day for baseball. With my shoes and glove tied over my handlebars, I biked over to the parking lot at Sampson Park. Everyone was there on bikes except Ollie, who'd be driving over with his dad, helping him carry the equipment bag. The rest of us set off on our bikes down Granger Avenue.

Cars gave our eight bikes a wide berth. I guess we must have been all over the street because everyone was talking to everyone else.

"We've never lost at Vets this year," Doodie said.

"We've never lost a postponed game either," Turner said.

"I hear Skanecki's got the flu," Jim Felch said.

"Who told you that?"

"Me. I was listening to my prayers."

"Haha."

"Hey, Randy, how does it feel to be in uniform again?"

"Awful."

"Don't feel that way, Randy. Skanecki said you were the one batter he was really scared of."

"How come?"

"He says Randy's due for a hit from the nine-year-old league."

"That's really funny. That's really the way to buck Randy up."

"Don't listen to them, Randy."

"I didn't hear a word."

Everyone laughed.

"Man, all you got to do is play as well as you coach."

"Remember Panello."

"That dude should have been on third on his own."

"Hey, I hear he's coming to the game."

"He's got a cast."

"My brother once played football with a hairline fracture."

"In his foot?"

"No, his arm."

"There's a difference."

"Yeah. The foot's below your waist, your arm's above it."

"Listen, don't nobody else get hurt."

"If we beat Baer today we play Cornish Wire next week."

"And then another shot at the Hardwares."

"Arch Wright gets back from vacation next week."

"Are you pitching today, Davey?"

"I don't know."

"Hey, you guys are going the wrong way. Let's go up Madison Street."

"Madison takes too long."

"Well, there's too much traffic on Huron."

"We'll race you there."

"OK, but everyone go at the same speed we're going now. No speeding up."

"Let's go, guys."

The minute we lost sight of the guys who were going on Huron, we speeded up. It was impossible not to. They must have done the same thing because when we got back on Huron where it meets with Seventh, they were a little bit ahead of us and pedaling like mad.

We raced all the way to Vets Park, and it was a pedal-weary, huffing-puffing bunch of Burton Bakers that arrived at sunbaked Vets. Mr. Stevens was there with Ollie, undoing the equipment bag. Some of the Baer Machine guys in orange caps and orange socks were there, throwing balls back and forth, loosening up. Already some onlookers had gathered in the bleachers. The diamonds at Vets Park are across the street from a big shopping center and a lot of men watch ball games while they wait for their wives to get through shopping.

Mr. Stevens took out some dark balls from the equipment bag and threw them at us. "Loosen up."

While we played catch, we traded insults with Baer Machine.

"You guys really blew it against the Hardwares, didn't you?"

"We decided to save it all up for you," Doodie said.

"I hear you got McElroy batting cleanup."

"You heard right, man. Only it's Teddy McElroy. We got special permission to use him cause of our broken leg."

"He's thirteen."

"Not anymore."

"Hey, Skanecki, you forgot to shave this morning."

"Say that at bat, Felch."

"How come you guys have never won on this diamond, Skanecki?"

"We decided to save it all up for you," Skanecki said with a grin, giving us back our own line.

"All right, let's have a little infield," Mr. Stevens called out. "Gehring on first, McElroy second, Stevens short, Brown third, Felch in left, Palwicz in right, Turner in center. Lundgren will be pitching today. Mark, you warm him up on the side. Throw easy, Dave. It's going to be a warm morning. OK, let's move out there. Dig. Hippity-hop to the barber shop. Go!"

We ran out on the field. Mr. Stevens went over to the bleachers. I saw him talk to my dad and Uncle Ned who had just arrived. They looked at each other, grinning, and then Uncle Ned gestured to Dad. Dad climbed out of the stands and got a catcher's mitt out of the equipment bag.

"Hey, your dad's going to catch for us," Otto said.

I nodded. I wasn't sure I liked it. No one would say anything but you'd have to be blind not to see a big difference in natural ability between father and son.

Mr. Stevens began hitting infield grounders, starting at third. I moved around nervously between first and second. I was at second because Davey was pitching and because Mr. Stevens must have figured I'd cause less harm here than in right. After all, if you let a ball go through your legs at second, you've got the right fielder backing you up. But if you're the right fielder and you let a ball go through you, all you've got behind you are the daisies, and they're not helpful.

"Wake up, Randy."

The dark practice ball came bouncing toward me. I knew my father was watching me closely. I stepped back. No, go in. I moved in, knocked it down, and threw to first.

A snotty cheer went up from the Baer Machines.

"A thing of beauty."

"You must have hired that guy. He's a professional."

"A professional tennis player. . . ."

"C'mon, Randy," Mr. Stevens said, "take charge of those balls. You play them, don't let them play you."

He hit a grounder to Otto who made the play himself, and a good thing too, because I'd forgotten I was supposed to cover first. Our pitchers never made it over from the mound. We weren't supposed to count on them.

Mr. Stevens hit some outfield flies and then we went around the infield again.

"Let's play for one. No errors. Here we go!"

This time when my turn came I made a clean play and I saw Dad nod approvingly. Dad looked great with the catcher's mitt. He scooped a couple of throws out of the dirt, and Mr. Stevens—just for a gag—when Dad flipped the ball to him, knocked it down with his hand. Dad pounced on it and fired it to Otto who yelled "Ouch. That hurt, Mr. McElroy."

"How come you don't throw like that, Randy?" Doodie asked.

"I don't want to hurt Otto's hand," I said.

"Let's play for two now," Mr. Stevens called out and knocked one down to third. Doodie charged it, grabbed it, and fired to me at second. It hurt my hand. My hands weren't callused. I threw it to first, awkwardly.

The Baer Machine kids razzed me. Ollie flipped me the next one for a short-to-second-to-first double play and this one I threw in the dirt at Otto.

"Let's try it again," Mr. Stevens called out. This time Ollie let the ball go through his legs.

The third time we clicked. Then we clicked on a second-to-short-to-first. By "clicked" I don't mean we could have gotten the batter out. I just mean we didn't throw the ball away. Then I even remembered to cover first when Otto came in to field a grounder.

"Way to go, Randy," Mr. Stevens called out.

Dad didn't say anything. He didn't say a thing when I goofed up or when I did OK. And that was how it should be. In the stands Uncle Ned watched silently, not missing a thing. I like to watch ball players watching a game. They never talk, and they see everything.

"OK," Mr. Stevens said, "let's get the guy at home."

Doodie fired it home. Dad caught it and winged it right back at him and we went around the horn.

Then Ollie fired it home and Dad pegged the ball back to second. I caught it and it stung my hand plenty and threw it back in the dirt. Dad scooped it up in one easy motion and glove-flipped it to Mr. Stevens. Everyone whistled.

Then I knocked the ball down at second and threw it home and Dad fired it at Ollie who fired it to Otto who fired it home.

The way Dad was winging that ball around was firing us up. Finally we brought the ball all the way in, fielding it, throwing it, and Dad would roll it back to us as we barehanded it back to him. Mr. Stevens did the same thing to the outfield and Dad brought them in with little grounders until we were all off the field and the Baer Machines had taken it over. We were huffing and puffing at our bench.

"Hey, Mr. McElroy, how'd you like to play for us?"

"You don't want me, Doodie," Dad said. "I'm an old third baseman."

Doodie grinned. "I'll move over to second."

Jim Felch turned to me. "Your dad must have been one helluva ball player."

"He was."

"How come you're so awful?"

"I wish I knew."

128

"Well, don't worry about it. Just do your best."

Jimmy slapped me on the back. He and I were good friends. Only a good friend can tell you how lousy you are to your face.

We watched Baer Machine go through infield practice. They were all right, but nothing like the Hardwares. No one was like the Hardwares. Take away Skanecki and the Baer Machines were nothing. With Skanecki, they could beat anyone.

On the sidelines, big Bob fired his swift one. Dad crooked a finger at me. I went over to him. "He's fast for his age, Randy, but those balls are coming straight in. They don't move on you. All you have to do is meet them. You don't even have to swing a lot. Choke up a little and bring your bat a little around and his speed will do the rest for you."

Dad made it sound simple. He always did. He had long ago convinced me that hitting was the simplest thing in the world—if you could do it.

"Good luck, Randy."

"Thanks."

He slapped me on the bottom and went back up in the bleachers and sat down with Uncle Ned. I watched them talk and Dad grin and I knew Uncle Ned was kidding him about his catching prowess.

I sat down on the bench and for the first time noticed Ray Panello there. Guys were autographing his cast.

"You too, Randy," he said.

"You're not sore at me then?"

"What for?"

They were all being nice to me. My welcome back to

the baseball wars was friendly. No one was sore, in fact no one seemed worried about anything, and that was a little scary. Here we'd lost a bitter heartbreaker to the Belden Hardwares, our number one pitcher only had two innings of eligibility left, we had a clown playing second base—by all rights we should be down in the dumps. But we weren't.

The sun was shining.

We were making wisecracks.

And Ray Panello, whose place I'd taken, whose leg was broken, was holding out his pen to me.

I wrote on his cast: "I wish this was on me. Randy McElroy."

Ray read it and laughed. "You'll be OK, Randy."

I hoped so. If I couldn't help this team, at least let me not hurt it.

"Batter up," the ump said.

12 · A TENSE BALL GAME

SKANECKI WAS IN great form. Big, sweating, grinning, tire-less—he challenged us with his fast-ball inning after in-ning. And down we went, pygmies and powerless.

By the fourth inning, he still had a no-hitter going. The closest anyone had come to a hit was a line drive by Mark Borker right back at the pitcher. Our only hope was that Skanecki would get tired. He threw hard all the time. And unlike Lonnie Malkus of the Hardwares, he didn't relax between pitches by talking to us.

"He just can't keep it up," Ollie said. "When he loses that edge we're gonna start hitting."

But that fast ball kept blasting in there and Mr. Stevens glumly informed us that Skanecki had all six innings of eligibility. Obviously, the Baer Machine coach had been saving him for us. This was as big a game for them as it was for us. The winner played the weak Cornish Wire team and was a cinch to get to the finals against the Hardwares.

While Skanecki had a no-hitter going, they were hitting Davey Lundgren in every inning, but good fielding and Davey coming through with clutch pitches in tough situations had kept them from scoring any runs.

It was a tense ball game, and when word got around Vets that a tight game was taking place on Diamond #1, the bleachers filled up. We must have had a hundred people watching us. Every now and then I'd glance over at my father and Uncle Ned. They watched the game silently, only once in a while speaking to each other. So far I was pleased with my performance. I'd done nothing to disgrace the McElroy name. True, I'd struck out my only time at bat, but so had a lot of other guys struck out. And I had the sense to go down swinging. In the field I hadn't made any mistakes but that was because not one ball had been hit my way. There had been a pop-up over second, but Ollie had moved over smoothly, called for it, and grabbed it.

The longer the game went this way the tenser it got, and quieter, as though guys were fearful of saying something that would get their side unhinged. I don't think I said a word out at second. I was scared to death that if I called out something like: "No stick in there, Davey," the batter would promptly hit a ball at me and I'd have to put up or shut up.

So because I had kept my mouth shut, no one had hit a ball to me. I'm usually not superstitious, but it was working. Every once in a while, to relieve the tension, I'd think about the river where you didn't have to catch the old bullhead in order to win. Just trying at the river was victory enough.

"C'mon, Randy. Let's move it, man."

Everyone was off the bench. It seemed we'd just sat down. I ran out to my position. If nothing else it would be a quick game, unless we went to extra innings. Then, I thought, we'd be in trouble. I knew Mr. Stevens was counting on Ollie to pitch the fifth and sixth innings, but if we went to extra innings who would pitch them? Steve? Bring back Davey? But then, the Baer Machines would be worse off. After Skanecki they only had that little left-hander. We never had trouble hitting him. So maybe extra innings was a good idea. Maybe it was the *only* idea.

"Wake up, Randy."

Otto rolled the ball to me. I picked it up and threw it back.

"C'mon, Randy," Ollie said, "pay attention."

I couldn't very well explain to them that I was paying attention. Not to infield practice but to what could happen in the later innings.

The Baer Machines had the big part of their lineup coming up in the bottom of the fourth. Tom Nettles, their first baseman, Skanecki, and Rob Franks their catcher. Davey walked around the mound, moving dirt around with the tips of his shoes. Pitchers are great landscapers.

133

They seem to believe that if they keep everything neat, no one will hit them.

Mark Borker squatted down. Ollie called out behind his glove: "Throw it by him, Davey. Be tough in there, Dave."

Nettles took a ball and then slapped a ground ball down the line at third. Doodie had to move fast just to get his glove on it. He knocked it down and then came the long throw to first. Nettles beat it out. A cheap infield hit. Davey spat. He wasn't the kind of pitcher who got fussed by bad breaks. He never thought of himself as a star hurler, just a guy who played second and threw the ball over the plate when the coach asked him to.

Davey had a good move to first, though I didn't figure Nettles to steal. He wasn't that fast, and besides Skanecki was a long ball hitter.

Ollie called out to me that he would take the throw if Nettles went down. Usually the second baseman takes the throw with a right-hand batter up, but it was a lot safer with Ollie taking it.

At bat, Skanecki didn't look as ferocious as he did on the mound, but he was a good hitter. In kids' baseball, the best ball players are always the pitcher, catcher, and shortstop. Often they're interchangeable. Catcher can pitch and pitchers can catch and both of them can play shortstop. The team that wins the championship is the team that has a few more good ball players in addition to the vital three. The Hardwares had nine good ball players. We had about six. The Baer Machines just had the three, and now the best of those three—the pitcher—was up.

Skanecki usually pulled the ball. I watched Jimmy take a few steps over to the foul line and Doodie, playing deep, moved toward the line.

Davey went to his stretch position, glanced at Nettles who only took a small lead, and then he threw to the plate. To my amazement, Skanecki bunted. Their number four hitter, their home run hitter, bunted down the first base line. Nettles was running by me. I looked at second. Ollie was cutting toward the bag. Where was I supposed to go? If I were sitting on the bench I'd be able to see it all, but out here in the middle of it, I didn't know. I froze . . . and it was only when Otto fielded the ball and turned to throw back to first that I realized I was supposed to be covering first.

Oh, you jackass, I thought.

I was afraid to look at the stands.

The Baer Machine bench was up and yelling. They had men on first and second and nobody out.

"Yo, ho, ho, here we go."

"They're coming apart. Give it a ride, Robby."

"Hey, Lundgren, you got no team behind you."

"Wait for your pitch, Robby baby."

Mr. Stevens was standing up, too. "You're watching the game, Randy," he said.

I nodded. My face was red. Uncle Ned and Dad looked grim.

Mark Borker was standing in front of the plate. "No one out," he said. "We got a play at third, second. Look alive, Doodie."

"I gotcha," Doodie said.

"Nobody out," the Baer Machine coach called out.

"Ducks on the pond, Robby," he said, and flashed what had to be a hit away sign at Rob Franks, their number five hitter. Franks was a big fat kid who hit long fly balls that occasionally fell between fielders. We could usually get him out.

"Hey, Pitcherpitcherpitcherpitcher," they shouted. "You're going upupupupup. . . ."

"No stick, Davey. Chuck away, Davey."

Davey showed no sign of being fussed by my mistake. He blew some bubble gum toward the batter, glanced over his shoulder at the runner on second, and then threw to the plate.

"Ball," the ump said.

"Hey, Pitcherpitcherpitcher. . . ."

"Stick with him, Davey boy."

"Chuck hard, Dave."

"Fat boy can't hit, Davey."

"He can hit you, Lundgren."

On the next pitch both runners broke. A double steal. I ran to second. Doodie broke for his bag . . . and they fooled us. Oh, how they fooled us. Rob Franks, fat and slow, bunted down the third base line. And there was absolutely no one there to field it. Davey had to come off the mound and by the time he picked it up everyone was safe.

The bleachers picked up the excitement of the Baer Machine bench. Lots of shouts and clapping. A tense ball game was breaking up. They could sense the kill coming. It was going to bust open now, like a thunderclap.

Mr. Stevens called time and came out to the mound. We gathered around.

"How're you feeling, Dave?"

"They ain't hit me solid yet," Davey said, and spat.

"That's right. All been luck so far. Well, keep them low on this next guy and we'll try for a play at the plate. This kid hasn't gotten a hit all season. Mark, give Davey a target around the knees so if he does hit it, it'll be on the ground. Infield, play in. We got to cut this run off. . . ."

He slapped Davey on the rump and the meeting broke up. Davey worked the bubble gum around in his mouth. We all said something to him and then we went back to our positions, only playing a lot closer in. Doodie was very close, so was Otto. I was back a little and so was Ollie. A pop fly would kill us. So would a hard-hit grounder, but those are the chances you have to take.

Their bench was having fits, yelling and gesturing. They knew their batter couldn't hit. They wanted to work Davey for a walk. The batter looked more scared than Davey. He looked like me up there. Any other time, I would have felt sorry for him.

Mark made a target and Davey threw, too low.

"He's gonna walk you, Charley."

"A walk's a run, Charley. A walk's an RBI, Charley."

"Wave your bat around, Charley."

"Look small up there, Charley."

Mark moved his target up. Davey's second pitch was right in there. A meatball. The kid's bat never left his shoulder.

All that talk about getting a walk wasn't doing the batter any good.

"No batter in there, Davey," I heard myself call out. "You're way ahead of him."

I'd broken my rule of not talking for fear of someone hitting the ball to me. But there was no chance this kid would swing. This kid at the plate was *their* Randy McElroy, a victim just like me.

Three men on, no one out, count one and one. Davey threw another pitch right down the middle. Another meatball. The kid hesitated. Someone yelled "Swing," and the kid swung—stiff and late. The ball hit off the end of his bat and came spinning right at me. Oh, dear God, please let me catch it. Please, please. . . .

I caught it cleanly.

"Home," Ollie yelled.

I threw it home as hard as I could.

"Out," the ump yelled.

Mark fired the ball to first. We should never have gotten that kid out at first, but he must have stayed around to watch the play at the plate, or else he was paralyzed because he hit the ball. It wasn't even close. A double play! I was just starting to feel proud and goose pimply and to look over at Dad and Uncle Ned in the bleachers when I heard Doodie scream.

"Home, Otto. Home!"

In the happy confusion of the double play, Skanecki was trying to sneak home. It was smart and daring.

Otto, who had been beaming proudly, just stared. Then he threw. Borker caught it. He had time to make the tag, but I guess something slipped in his mind. He didn't make a tag at all. He just caught it with one foot on home plate, and I knew instantly he had forgotten Skanecki was not forced. That first runner coming home had been forced, but not Skanecki. But we had talked so much about a force play at the plate that Mark just had a lapse. Skanecki slid in, untouched.

"Safe," the ump shouted, and to Mark who looked at him bewildered, he said: "He wasn't forced, catcher."

Mark just stood there, baffled, and then he realized what he'd done. I thought for a second he was going to cry. He swallowed and walked out to the mound.

"Davey, I'm . . . sorry."

Davey shook his head. "We'll get it back, Mark." He turned to me. "Nice playing, Randy."

"Yeah," Ollie said, "that was a good play, Randy."

And Mr. Stevens called out. "We'll get that one back, boys. Nice playing out there."

It was funny. The one good play I'd ever made was followed by a bonehead play by one of our steadiest players. It was like you could only improve at the expense of someone else. A crazy game, baseball.

I didn't know whether to feel good or bad. Good because I'd made a good play, or bad because we were now a run behind.

One thing though, I wouldn't be afraid any longer to talk it up behind Davey.

"No stick, Davey," I heard myself say quietly.

Davey got the third out on a pop-up to third, and we were in for the top of the fifth. Six outs away from defeat by a team we should be beating.

13 · "WHY DID IT HAVE TO BE YOU, McELROY?"

"OK, GUYS," Mr. Stevens said, "let's get it back. Felch, Gehring, Turner, Borker. Jimmy, you get on base and we'll bring you around."

Easier said than done against big Bob Skanecki. He had only a one-run lead but the way he was pitching it might as well have been ten. Jim and Mr. Stevens had a quick conference and then Jim tossed away the red doughnut and went up to the plate.

"C'mon, guys," Ollie said, "let's talk it up."

"Hey, Pitcherpitcherpitcher. . . ."

"Give it a rap, Jim. He's getting tired."

Skanecki wound up and pitched to the plate. Jim squared around to bunt. The ball went up in the air. An easy out as the catcher grabbed it a foot in foul territory. Jimmy slammed his bat down in disgust.

"C'mon, Otto, you can do it. He's getting tired."

That was wishful thinking, I thought.

Otto looked grim up at the plate. He had an unorthodox batting stance. He was a big guy who went into a corkscrew position. I guess he felt comfortable in it. All I knew was that he had a good eye and always made contact with the ball. He hit a lot of soft liners that dropped in for singles.

Skanecki got two quick blistering strikes on him. I don't think Otto even saw the ball. I know I didn't.

"Hang tough, Otto."

"Protect that plate."

"Only takes one to do it."

"He's scared of you, Bob."

"He won't swing, Bob."

But Otto did swing. On the very next pitch. Anxious to protect the plate against fast balls he could barely see, Otto swung at the next pitch which was a foot over his head.

"Whee. . . ." The Baer Machines shouted, as they winged the ball around the infield Otto returned to the bench and buried his face in his hands. No one said a thing to him.

Steve Turner was next up; he choked way up on the bat.

"Spoil it for him, Steve," Ollie cried.

"How?" Doodie mumbled.

"Get hit by a pitch," Jim Felch said, "that's how."

"Not by one of those fast balls," Doodie said.

Steve managed to work Skanecki for a couple of balls before he took a strike. And then he fooled everyone, including Mr. Stevens, by laying down a bunt. It was a good idea, but the ball came off his bat too hard and Skanecki was able to field it and throw him out.

It didn't look good. We weren't getting any breaks.

Mr. Stevens stopped Davey on his way out to the mound. "Can you give me another inning?"

Davey blew a bubble. "Sure."

This meant we'd have Ollie for an extra inning or two in case Davey got tired, and, what was more unlikely, in case we got into extra innings. We had the bottom of the batting order coming up in our last licks. Skanecki was pitching a perfect game.

Davey had the bottom of their order right now, and like the bottom of most teams they kept their bats on their shoulders and waited for walks. Davey was stingy with walks. You could get on base against him but you had to earn it. He struck out the first two guys and their last man grounded out short to first. We came running in for the top of the sixth, and our last licks.

"Borker, Palwicz, McElroy," Mr. Stevens called out. "You can hit this guy, Mark. You've hit him best so far."

He was recalling Mark's line drive in the third inning. As I watched Mark take off his shin pads I wondered what he was thinking about: his line drive in the third inning or his mental lapse at the plate in the fourth.

142

Mark was the logical one to be able to hit a fast ball pitcher. He swung with a choked bat and had a small controlled swing. It was only his second time up, as it would be mine. That's the way a perfect game against you goes—fast. Though later, when you remember it, it stretches out miserably in time.

"Swing a bat, Randy," Ollie ordered me.

I got up, picked out a light Lou Brock special, and swung it.

Out at the mound Skanecki was sweating, but the more he sweated the looser he got. It didn't seem possible a kid only eleven years old could pitch that long and that hard without getting tired, but there he was pouring that fast one over, challenging us, and beating us.

Mark took a ball and then a strike and then he swung and made good contact with the ball, but again he hit it right at someone—the left fielder. Still, the sound of his bat against the ball was the most encouraging sound we'd heard all morning. This was also the first ball we'd hit out of the infield.

It woke us up a little.

Ed Palwicz stepped in. The Baer Machine sensed the end now. Only two outs away from victory and the two weakest hitters on the team coming up. Skanecki was only two outs away from a perfect game: no hits, no walks, no errors.

Skanecki wheeled and delivered . . . high for a ball.

"Good eye, Ed."

"Make him pitch to you, Ed."

"He's getting weary. Hey, Skanecki, you're getting tired."

Palwicz, tall and serious, never took his eye off Skanecki. The next pitch was low for a ball. Was Skanecki
really tiring? I'd seen it happen before. A guy going from
looking great to falling apart in fifteen seconds. If Ed
could work him for a walk, that meant some of the pressure would be off me. Unless I hit into a double play, I
wouldn't have to be the last out in the game. Stop it, I
said to myself, stop worrying about yourself.

I looked over at my father and Uncle Ned. They were
watching with intense concentration. I was just another
kid in a baseball uniform to them, I hoped.

Mr. Stevens put a take sign on to Ed and Ed took the
next pitch for a strike. That relaxed the Baer Machine
coach. I glanced at their third baseman. He moved back a
step. Ed never bunted, but if ever there was a time for a
bunt it was now, I thought.

I heard myself suddenly call out: "You know what to
do, Ed."

It was dumb and didn't mean a thing, but for some reason Ed glanced at me swinging a bat and in that glance I
know he saw the third baseman moving back. Skanecki
pumped, reared back, and threw. Ed bunted. It caught
them flatfooted. Skanecki hustled for it, the third baseman came running in, and then they both hesitated, fear-
ing a collision, and that was our first break in the game.
Skanecki finally picked it up but it was too late. Ed was
across first with a bunt single, the perfect game was ru-
ined.

We were all yelling. Skanecki walked slowly back to
the mound. I felt sorry for him but I was also starting to
feel sorry for myself. He'd be doubly tough on me.

144

"Hold on, Randy," Mr. Stevens said. He came over to me. Put his arm around me. "Take a pitch and lay it down to third."

I nodded. It was the right move. Davey Lundgren was a good hitter. A single would tie up the game if I could get Ed to second. Ed wasn't too fast; he wouldn't be stealing. So I had to deliver him to second.

I wiped my hands on my pants. They were wet. They hadn't been wet a second ago. I looked up and there were Dad and Uncle Ned looking at me. I looked away.

Take a pitch and lay it down. Take a pitch and lay it down. I repeated the words in my mind.

"C'mon, Batter, let's get up there."

I stepped in. I knew our bench was shouting and their team, too, but I couldn't hear a word either of them said. I did hear Rob Franks, their catcher, saying softly, almost to himself: "Fire away, Big Bob. No hitter here. Fire away, Big Bob."

For the first time in the game, Skanecki had to pitch from a stretch position. Ed Palwicz didn't take much of a lead. Skanecki threw to the plate.

"Strike," the ump called.

That ball had really zipped by me. Lay it down? How do you bunt a ball you can't see?

I choked up a little. Take a pitch and lay it down. Take a pitch and lay it down.

Skanecki checked Palwicz and then fired toward me. I squared around. I offered my bat to the ball but the ball didn't come near it.

"Strike two," the ump said.

"Step out of the box, Randy," Mr. Stevens called down to me.

My heart was pounding. I had to get myself together. Two strikes and no balls. I looked to Mr. Stevens. He gave me the hit away sign. Hit away? Hit what away?

I wiped my hands again. Skanecki was watching me, a half-grin on his face. I was still his meat and he knew it. I wasn't a ball player; I was a fisherman. No, don't think about fishing now. Think about what you've got to do.

"Let's go, Batter," the ump said.

"McElroy doesn't want to bat," their shortstop yelled.

I rubbed some dirt on my hands and as I stepped in I knew there was only one way for me to move Ed from first to second and that was to get hit by the ball. This was how the season had started for me. I'd failed then but now I had to succeed. It was the only way. Even if it hurt. And from Skanecki it would hurt.

"Come on, McElroy, get in there," Skanecki called down to me. "I won't bite you."

Laughter. If you bite me, I thought, I'll be on first and Ed will be on second. Bite me, Skanecki. Please bite me.

Skanecki looked in for his sign. He had only one pitch but he always took a sign for it.

I crowded the plate. My left elbow was up—over the plate.

His right arm flashed high in the air. I saw a glimpse of white in his hand and then that white ball was screaming through the air at me. It was inside. High and inside. A perfect pitch. All I had to do was hold my ground, stick in there. It would hit me on the left shoulder. I was too slow to get out of the way.

146

But something snapped inside. At the last second I chickened out. I swerved to get out of the way, falling to my left. What happened next I recall in a kind of numbness. The bat stung my hands. Pain shot up my wrists and arms, but I didn't know what had happened. Everyone was yelling. And then through the noise and din I heard one voice clear and sharp. It was Dad's.

"Run, Randy, run!" he yelled.

I didn't even know where the ball was, but I started running. I took off for first base and it was only when I got there that I saw where the ball had gone. It was rolling along the left field foul line, in fair territory, and their left fielder, who had been shaded way over to center figuring me to swing late if I swung at all, was running hard, chasing it down. As I was trying to avoid getting hit by the pitch, the ball had hit my bat. I had pulled it down the left field foul line. Ed Palwicz was coming into third base and I saw Mr. Stevens waving him home.

The Baer Machines were yelling frantically to their left fielder to throw it home. I took off for second. I'd never made it to second as a base runner in a league game.

As I got to second, there was a play on Ed at the plate. The catcher had it and then he didn't have it. It was through him, behind him, he turned and was running for it. I took off for third.

Mr. Stevens was screaming at me, waving me to keep on going. As I headed into third I looked to the plate. The catcher didn't have the ball yet. What should I do? I looked at Mr. Stevens. The thought crossed my mind that I was making the same mistake Ray Panello had made.

"Keep going, Randy," Mr. Stevens screamed, and I

did, but I'd lost valuable seconds. I made my turn and ran for home. The catcher had found the ball. Skanecki was covering home plate, his back to me. He was yelling for the ball.

"Run, Randy. Run," my teammates shouted.

I ran as hard as I could. The catcher threw the ball. Skanecki had it now, he was turning to face me. Everyone was screaming. And then I heard Dad again, loud and clear:

"Slide, Randy, slide."

I slid immediately. I launched myself into what became known for years later as Randy McElroy's great slide. I must have been at least fifteen feet from home plate when I slid. I slid and slid and slid. By the time I reached Skanecki I was all slid out. I just lay there, a foot short of the plate.

Grinning, Skanecki merely had to reach over and tag my toe. Which he did.

"You're out," the ump said, and started laughing.

And then I heard the laughter from the stands. Grown-up laughter. I lay there feeling naked and stupid, and then I was aware that six or seven baseball players had jumped off our bench and were running toward me. I knew they had every reason to be sore at me for that dumb slide, but I was going to defend myself just the same.

I doubled up my fists and then before I could swing they were all over me: Doodie, Davey, Ollie, Jimmy, smacking me, and Otto giving me a big wet kiss on the cheek.

"You did it, Randy."

148

"You saved it, man."

"Oh, Randy. . . ."

They weren't sore at me at all. They were congratulating me.

"We're tied," Ollie said, jumping up and down, "and Skanecki is all through after this inning. It's curtains for them now. Way to go, Randy. Way to go."

Nobody was mad at me. In the stands Uncle Ned was telling Dad something and Dad was grinning, embarrassed, and Uncle Ned was laughing. The guys dusted me off and hauled me back to the bench.

Skanecki got Davey Lundgren out on a pop-up, but it was curtains for them after that. Ollie came in to pitch the bottom of the sixth and mowed them down in order. And then in the top of the seventh, they brought in their little left-hander, and bats that Skanecki had silenced for six innings now began to sing out.

Doodie started things off by hitting a triple between left and center. Ollie singled him home. Jim Felch then blasted a home run over the left fielder's head. By the time the inning was over we had four big runs. A tense game was now a shambles. We were winning 5-1.

In the bottom of the seventh, Ollie set them down one, two, three. The game ended on a strikeout. And we ran to the mound shrieking like wild Indians. Everyone started pounding everyone else. Mr. Stevens ran out and kissed Davey Lundgren and hugged me and I pounded Davey and Davey pounded me and Ollie was jumping on everyone's back and Jimmy Felch wanted us to carry *him* off because of his homer and it was a general mess of happiness.

Finally, Mr. Stevens brought it to an end. "OK, let's go over and shake hands. This was a tough one for them to lose. Skanecki pitched his heart out. Shake hands and no wisecracks from anyone."

We wiped the grins off our faces and tried to look solemn when we said: "Good game," to the Baer Machines and held out our hands. A couple of them were actually crying. Most of them wouldn't shake hands with us. I came up to Skanecki. He was standing there, a towel around his neck. He looked exhausted. He looked at me a second, then shook hands and asked: "Why did it have to be you, McElroy?"

I didn't know what to say to that, so I didn't say anything. I told him he pitched a great game and I'd enjoy watching him pitch in the majors some day.

"Yeah," he said, shrugged, and walked away.

Then it was my father and Uncle Ned climbing down from the stands. They shook hands with Mr. Stevens and congratulated Davey and Ollie and Jimmy, and then they came over to me.

Uncle Ned was grinning. "I told your dad to stop coaching from the stands, Randy. Next time he yells 'slide,' wait a couple of seconds."

Dad blushed. He ran his fingers through my hair. "That was quite a hit, son," he said. He looked at me and I looked at him, and then we both laughed, and Uncle Ned did too. I don't know whether he thought my hit was funny or wonderful and maybe it didn't matter at all. He and Uncle Ned had had a good time at a ball game, which was what baseball was all about anyway.

"You coming home with us?" Dad asked.

"No. I've got my bike. I'm going back with the guys."

"We'll see you at the house then."

"Dad, is it OK if I go fishing this afternoon?"

"Sure, it's OK." I think he knew what I was thinking. A great piece of luck had hit me on the diamond, maybe it would also hit me at the river. Today might be THE DAY. If I, Randy McElroy could bat in a run off Bob Skanecki, then I, Randy McElroy, could also catch the oldest, smartest, biggest bullhead that ever swam in a Michigan river.

"By the way, you're going to help me brush up on my fly fishing. Your uncle and I have a bet on who'll catch more trout up north this summer. He claims he can outfish me with his eyes closed, so. . . ."

Crazy, just crazy. We win a big ball game and Dad ends up talking about fishing. This had to be the biggest victory.

14 · END OF A SEASON: END OF A STORY

WELL, MY STORY really ends here. I did not catch the old bullhead that afternoon. I tried long and hard with the green frog lure the old fisherman from Ohio had given me. But I guess the old bullhead heard this was my lucky day. I didn't get a bite. I didn't even get to see him.

On Monday we played Cornish Wire in the playoffs and beat them. On Wednesday we played the Hardwares for the championship and lost 5-3. I didn't play in either game. Archie Wright was back from vacation and I asked Mr. Stevens's permission not to suit up. I wanted to quit while I was ahead. He let me coach third in both games and I guess I did OK. At least no one broke a leg.

Labor Day weekend, when everyone got back from vacation, Mr. and Mrs. Stevens gave a team picnic in Sampson Park and while the hamburgers were cooking we lay in the grass and talked.

Naturally the talk turned to next spring when the diamonds would be bigger and the pitchers would be throwing curves. We'd be drafting new players from teams that dissolved and everyone was saying how Baer Machine might break up and we'd have a chance to get Skanecki.

Otto asked if I was going to play next season and I told him no. "My baseball days are over," I announced.

Mr. Stevens was amused. "So you're going to retire at the age of eleven, Randy?"

"Yes, sir. Of course if you ever need a hot pinch hitter. . . ."

They laughed. But then Ollie got serious. "You know something," he said. "I'm gonna miss Randy. That game against Baer Machine . . . I'll never forget it as long as I live."

"Me neither," Doodie said.

"That was one great game."

"And Randy saved it for us. Remember?"

They started reliving that crazy sixth inning with Ed on first and me not trying to get hit by the pitch and driving the ball over third base and sliding when my dad told me to slide, fifteen feet short of the plate.

"I'll say this," Ollie said, "Randy may be the worst baseball player in our league, but I'm gonna miss him just the same."

"I'm gonna miss you too, Randy," Doodie said.

"Me too—" Davey.

"Me too—" Turner and Borker and Otto, Jimmy, Ed, Ray. . . .

I waited till they were done making themselves feel so good and generous. They were really bathing in it. When they had finished, I said, without smiling:

"Gee, maybe I *will* play again next year."

There was a moment of startled silence. Finally I burst into laughter. And they piled on me. We had a real free-for-all in the grass that ended only when Mr. Stevens called out: "Do you kids want to pile on Randy or eat hamburgers?"

"Hamburgers," we all shouted together, and ran for the food.

ABOUT THE AUTHOR

Alfred Slote lives in Ann Arbor, Michigan, where he is active in Little League coaching, playing squash, and writing books for young people. He has also taught English at Williams College. Among his other books are STRANGER ON THE BALL CLUB and JAKE. Mr. Slote and his wife have three sports-minded children.